Evening at Tony's

Barbara Ann Carle

Inklings Publishing
Houston, Texas

Published by Inklings Publishing, Houston, Texas
https://www.inklingspublishing.com/

Development Editing: Max Regan of Hollowdeck Press
Copyediting: Ann Kellett
Editorial Review: Rachel Connelly
Cover Design: Arthur Doweyko
Interior Design: Erika Q. Stokes

ISBN: 978-1-944428-46-4 (Print)
978-1-944428-47-1 (e-book)

Dedication

In 1956, I met a tall, handsome, blond engineer who asked me out on a date. I made the smartest decision of my life the day I said, "Yes." Together, we have lived the greatest true love story ever. I dedicate this book to the man who always makes me laugh and who holds me whenever I cry. He is my real Knight in Shining Armor, my husband, Ed.

Louis

"Good evening. Welcome to Tony's. Do you have a reservation?"

I wonder how many times I've said those words. I started at Tony's long before I was old enough to be a full-time employee. The original owners, Tony and his wife, Carmen—affectionately known by everyone as Mama—were friends of my mother. Knowing she was a widow, raising a strapping, thirteen-year-old boy all on her own, Tony thought it would be a good idea to hire me for odd jobs around the place. Each week he gave me a schedule of deliveries he was expecting. If I kept my grades up, I was to show up and help unload boxes off the trucks. Once a week, Tony handed me a small envelope. Inside was a list of the dates and the hours I had worked, together with the amount of money I had earned. In addition, Mama never let me leave the restaurant without a huge package of what she called "left-over" food. It wasn't until I got older that I realized they probably weren't really leftovers. I can't tell you how proud I felt when I handed my mom that first envelope and package of food.

The original Tony's was a completely different place, a typical Italian restaurant, red-and-white checkered tablecloths, empty Chianti wine bottles converted into candle holders in the center of each table. Tony's friend from the old country, Victor, had painted murals of Rome on two walls and an amazing replica of their village back in Italy across the far wall.

We were open for lunch in those days. I'm trying to talk Anthony into revisiting that idea. I know his son has applied to some pretty expensive universities and the increase in revenue might help Anthony. The bar used to be part of the main dining room, and lots of Tony's friends would sit there for hours drinking and talking about the old country. We even had a jukebox and occasionally they'd sing along with Mario Lanza and Enrico Caruso. Business was always good thanks to Mama's famous cooking. Best Italian food in town.

By the time I was fifteen, I was already their weekend busboy and working full-time during the summer. Tony's oldest son, Dominick, started bussing tables that summer too. I could tell right away that he didn't like the work. It was obvious Tony was grooming him to take over the business, showing Dominick how this worked or how to do that. But Dominick just didn't care.

Two years later—I was waiting tables by then—their youngest son, Anthony, came to bus my station. Now, that kid was different. Nearly drove me crazy with his questions.

"Louis, how many tables do you turn over each night?"

"Louis, how many bottles of red wine do we order a week?"

I'd say, "Ask your father."

And he'd say, "My dad told me to ask you."

I knew Tony was just trying to get rid of him. He was probably just as tired of answering all the kid's questions. He worked with me for only two summers before he was waiting tables too. He got to know all our regulars by name. The customers loved him; he was friendly and efficient. When he was a senior in high school, he was already helping Tony with the books and had reorganized most of the restaurant. When he went off to college, everybody missed him, even the customers.

After graduating, he came home full of ideas on how to improve the restaurant.

"We need to computerize, Pop." Anthony said.

"Pop, we need to modernize."

"We need to go out for bids. I know we can get our alcohol cheaper."

But the old man was old world and stubborn, and argued Anthony down every time, no matter what Mama said. For a while I was afraid Anthony was gonna go work somewhere else. But he really loved his dad and always gave in. As the old couple got up in years, Anthony eventually took over management of the restaurant. By then, Anthony and I had become good friends. Soon, I was like his right-hand man. I handled the waiters and helped Anthony any way I could.

Everyone was devastated when Mama passed, especially Tony. He seemed to lose his heart when he lost her. He still spent every day at the restaurant, but he just sat at the table over by the kitchen. He didn't interact with the customers anymore. Two years later, he was gone too. Anthony took losing his parents really hard.

I have to be honest. I didn't know what was gonna happen after the old man died. Dominick was a big lawyer by then and had absolutely no interest in the restaurant, but he was the oldest son. Did Tony leave him the business? Would Dominick let Anthony keep running the place? Dominick and Anthony were close, so we all hoped things would turn out okay. But when it comes to money, you never know.

Everyone was pleasantly surprised, especially Dominick, when they read the will. Tony had left Anthony the restaurant and Dominick the house.

Anthony told me Dominick gave him a huge hug and said, "Thank God he didn't leave me the place. I hated it. I was always after them to sell it and retire, enjoy their later years. Every time I visited, they were so busy working, they couldn't even sit down and talk to me for more than ten or fifteen minutes at the most. The only time they seemed to rest was on the holidays, and even than Mama was doing all the cooking. And, Anthony, you're just like them." He laughed.

Anthony mourned for over two years. And then one day I walked into his office and his desk was covered with plans.

"What's this?" I asked.

"These are my ideas for the new restaurant. Come sit, I'll show you them."

He explained we'd have to close for a few months. The new restaurant was going to be warm, welcoming—everything he ever dreamed of. He described dark mahogany paneling, walls painted deep green. The carved, wooden bar decorated with old-fashioned brass trim would be in a separate area. There would also be brass lighting throughout, starched white linens, real china, sterling silver, crystal, and waiters in uniforms. That's when I started to worry. I was fifty years old. He wouldn't need or want an old guy like me around in his fancy, new restaurant. I decided I'd hang around as long as I could and help him until his project was completed.

So, we closed. Construction would have been a nightmare if it wasn't for Anthony. He was there every day, overseeing everything. And the place turned out amazing, more old-world than modern. He even kept Victor's big mural of their village in Italy on the back wall. I helped him interview and hire the staff. I even helped plan the new menu, picking out which of Mama's most popular dishes to include. As opening night drew closer, I planned my speech. Quitting was going to be the hardest thing I ever had to do. But Anthony beat me to it.

"About you, Louis," he started.

"You don't have to worry about me, Anthony," I interrupted. "I understand. I've already started looking for another job. You need young people working around here." I finished and looked at Anthony.

He leaned back in his chair and stared at me.

"You're an idiot," he said, shaking his head.

"If you had let me finish, I would have told you that I want you to go get fitted for a jacket. A maître d' should wear a jacket, don't you think? Did you really think I was gonna let you go after all this time, Louis? You're Rickie's godfather, for God's sakes. Did you and your mom—God rest her soul—ever miss a single holiday dinner at our house? You and me, we've been running Tony's for how many years now? And you thought I would, all of a sudden, toss you aside and start running this place on my own. Jeez!"

He jumped up out of his seat, grabbed me, and gave me a bone-cracking hug. I've got to admit, I cried. I guess he was right, I was an idiot.

I arrived at the restaurant this morning before Anthony. That's the second time this week I've had to open up. It's a game we've played over the years, a game he usually wins. As I walk through the dining room checking the tables, I'm happy to see what good shape everything is in. We have a really good crew. They don't try to rush out after closing. They take their time, making sure their stations are shipshape before they go home.

When Anthony finally shows up, he looks annoyed.

I'm standing behind the bar where I've just brewed a pot of coffee.

"Sorry I'm late," he says. "Maria's car wouldn't start. It was the battery, so I had to go pick one up at the auto parts store and install it. You know how much I hate it when you win twice in one week." He laughs and sits on one of the bar stools.

"No problem, boss." I smile and hand Anthony his first cup of the day, one of many to come. The boss loves his coffee.

"Thanks, Louis. How does it look for tonight?" He takes a sip.

"We're already pretty booked up. It is Saturday," I say with a smile.

"That's good, except they're forecasting rain. I hate it when it rains. We'll be okay, as long as it doesn't pour." Anthony frowns.

"We'll be fine. Business has been really good this year."

"Yeah, knock on wood. We need to start planning for the holidays, make sure we've placed all our orders. Can you believe Thanksgiving is just nineteen days away? Do you want me to coordinate with the chef?"

"No, I'll do that, boss. We placed all our orders two months ago. He gave me a last-minute list two weeks ago. But I'll go over everything with him again," I assure him.

"Thanks. I can't believe it's that time of year again so soon," Anthony sighs. "You're bringing Anna for Thanksgiving, aren't you?"

"I guess. I haven't asked her yet."

"She's come over every Thanksgiving for the last five years, and you still ask her, like it's some kind of date or something. When are you gonna marry Anna, Louis?" Anthony gives me that look that means he's serious.

"I don't know. Remember, once I mentioned marriage, and she said she wasn't interested." I sigh.

"Louis, that was three years ago. She didn't break up with you, did she? Is she seeing other men?"

"No," I answer, hoping for some way to change the subject.

"Five years and she's still going out with you. I think she's probably changed her mind by now." He shakes his head.

"I've been a bachelor my whole life. I'm too old to get married," I say, and fold my arms across my chest.

"Do you know that old folks' home that Maria volunteers at? Last week they had a wedding there and the groom was ninety years old. I don't think you're too old to get married. Do you love Anna?" Anthony asks me seriously.

"Of course I do. I wouldn't be going with her all this time if I didn't."

"You love her. We love her. Look, just call Maria. Talk to her, she'll level with you. She's always easy to talk to. And remember, Christmas is a great time to get engaged," he says with a laugh.

"Okay, okay, Anthony," I say. "Now let's get back to business. I'll also check with the chef about tomorrow. Remember, we have the DeMarco seventieth wedding anniversary party. They've booked over half of our tables."

"How about staff? Do we have enough workers scheduled? Rickie is available if you need him."

"I think we're all right. Remember, we asked everyone to come in a couple of hours early to help set up, and we're paying them overtime," I say, even though I'm sure he remembers.

"No problem. I want everything to go smoothly. Who from the family is handling the arrangements?"

"Their youngest son, Eric."

"We went to school together. Be sure to tell him we'll comp the wine," he says emphatically.

"You sure, Anthony? That's gonna cost us," I say uneasily.

"Louis. That whole family has been eating here since Mom and Pop opened the place. They've been good customers all these years. I also want us to pay for the cake. The family will appreciate it. And it will be good for business." He smiles.

We hear laughter from the back as the staff begins to arrive.

"Well, sounds like they're in a good mood," I laugh.

The phone out front rings and I head for my lectern.

"Good afternoon," I say. "You've reached Tony's Restaurant. How may I help you?"

Nona

"HAPPY BIRTHDAY TO YOU! HAPPY BIRTHDAY, DEAR NONA. HAPPY BIRTHDAY TO YOU."

I smile and gaze at my five laughing best friends, the empty chair, and Keith. I try to act happy. But how happy can you be about your thirty-second birthday when you still live at home with your parents, you hate your boss, you haven't been in a relationship in over two years and, in fact, you haven't been in a *decent* relationship in longer than that?

"Hey Nona, should we call the fire department to help you blow out the candles?" Keith calls from the end of the table.

Everyone else just groans but I yell back, "Very funny, Keith."

We made our reservation for early evening to avoid the crowds, since it is Saturday. And we wanted the long table over in the corner. I hope the singing and our laughter won't disturb too many customers. All of us are regulars here and wouldn't want to hurt their business.

Just then, Louis, the maître d', walks over and says, "Did I hear people singing 'Happy Birthday' for you, Nona?! Hope you have many more, my friend."

"Thanks, Louis, I hope we're not making too much noise?"

"Don't be silly! People come to Tony's to have a good time. You guys have fun. By the way, how is Mr. Perkins doing?" he asks.

"Oh, he's fine. We've been pretty busy lately, but I'll be calling you next week to schedule the executive team's Christmas party," I say with a laugh.

"Well, sounds good to me." He smiles and walks away.

Loretta, my soul sister, indicating the empty seat, says, "He still may show up."

"You shouldn't have invited him. He hardly knows any of us. He's not even in our department," I say.

"That's the point! This is his perfect opportunity to get to know everybody better, especially you," Loretta grins.

"You have got to stop playing matchmaker for me. I think Mr. Superhero is way out of my league. He's from the Justice League and I'm from the Mediocre League," I laugh.

"Will you stop it? You're beautiful. All that long, wavy blond hair, those big blue eyes—you're gorgeous!"

"Yeah, I guess if he's into an aging, overweight, Christie Brinkley lookalike," I chuckle.

Everyone at the table makes up the accounting department at Empire, Inc. Loretta, Mary Jo, Dena, and I do the actual accounting, plus anything else the company decides to throw our way. Walter and Nate are our tech guys. What they don't know about computers hasn't been invented yet. And then there's Keith. Keith does practically nothing. He's rarely around, which is fine with us. The other member of our department isn't here tonight—our boss, Peter Jones. That's because Peter wasn't invited. He never is.

The empty chair is reserved for the newest hire at Empire, Inc. The day the owner introduced the muscular, tall, dark, and handsome Taylor Miles, at our monthly luncheon, Loretta texted me from her cell, which she had hidden under the conference table.

> OMG. He's a freakin' superhero. Look at the square jaw. He's come to save the day! Maybe we can get him to take on the villainous Peter Jones.

I immediately texted back.

> Ha, ha. You're a nut. But he does look like a superhero.

Now, Loretta kicks me under the table and quickly moves over one seat so that the vacant chair is next to me. I'm confused until I see Taylor Miles making his way towards our table.

He smiles as he sits down next to me and says, "I'm sorry I'm so late. I had a previous commitment that delayed me."

"You just missed the singing, which was probably a blessing. They're not exactly the Mormon Tabernacle Choir," I smile.

"Hey, Taylor!" calls Keith. "Switch seats with Loretta. You don't want to sit next to 'No, No, Nona'." He makes quotation signs with his fingers and laughs. "You need to be down here with us guys."

"Shut up, Keith." Walter says. Walter leans closer and whispers to him, "You're such an ass."

Keith swivels around and gives Walter that pouty look he's mastered over the years whenever someone pushes back at him. I just smile at Walter.

"Thanks, Keith," Taylor says. "I'm fine right where I am." He turns to me and says, "So, Keith is that guy."

"What guy?" I ask in all innocence.

"The guy everyone loves to hate," he says with a laugh.

"Well, he is the owner's nephew."

"Ah, that explains everything. So, how old are you today, or am I not supposed to ask that question?" Taylor smiles.

I stare at the giant three and two sitting among numerous single candles on the top of the cake and wonder if I could claim they accidentally reversed the numbers and I'm really twenty-three. But I know there's no way I can pull that off.

"I turn thirty-two tomorrow. And you should never ask a lady her age, just for future reference," I laugh.

"Oh, sorry, but I think thirty-two is the perfect age for a woman," Taylor says, looking serious.

"You do?" I wonder if this is a line he uses often or if he means it.

"Yes. I mean, you're finally old enough to know what you want out of life."

"You are? I mean. *Yes, of course.*" I try to sound positive.

"Well, personally speaking, I didn't have a clue in my twenties. I worked for several companies all over Europe. Basically, I bummed around, changing jobs just on a whim. It wasn't until I was in my early thirties that I knew where I was going with my life. I finally wanted to settle down, get serious and make something of myself. Maybe even get married."

"Bumming around Europe, yeah, that sounds rough," I say. "I've never been anywhere. I've never even left this state." I smile, shaking my head and brushing my hair away from my face.

"Well, that's what vacations are for," he says with a smile.

Taylor Miles has obviously operated at a different socio-economic level than I have.

"You've forgotten one thing. You need money to do that." I smile.

"How long have you worked for Empire, Inc.?" he asks, ignoring my remark about money.

"I started as a summer student during my senior year in college. They offered me a job after graduation," I say, realizing how boring that sounds.

"You must really love your job."

"Empire is a great company. I think you'll really like working here. We have great benefits, and the company has a solid future." I sound like a company brochure.

"How about your job? Do you love it? You work for Peter Jones, don't you? I've heard some rumors about him."

"Look, I'm not into gossip," I say, not liking where this conversation is headed. "You're new to the company and I'm happy to tell you anything about the company itself, but I don't talk about individuals."

"Hey, Nona!" Keith calls out. "Since you're such a special friend of the maître d', Maybe you can get him to comp some ice cream to go with the cake."

"No, Keith," I reply. "If you want ice cream with your cake, you're gonna have to pay for it yourself."

"Well, I just thought, since you two are so close, and all," Keith responds, wiggling his eyebrows.

"Shut up, Keith," Walter says again.

"What is that all about?" Taylor asks.

"Mr. Perkins likes to host gatherings for the company's executives here, what I like to call 'atta-boy nights'. Also, dinner parties to celebrate a successful year, the closing of a big sale, etc. So, we're a pretty good customer. I'm in charge of organizing all company events, the Christmas party, the annual picnics. So, over the years, I've worked a lot with Louis, the maître d'. He stopped by to wish me a happy birthday. Naturally, Keith thinks we should get some free ice cream. *Arrg!"* I growl.

"But I thought you headed up the Accounting Department," Taylor says, looking confused.

"I do, but we're a small company, getting bigger all the time. And the bigger we get, more and more small jobs are passed on to our department. Like we now make all travel arrangements for the executives and the sales department. Not exactly an accounting function," I say with a laugh.

"Keith works in your department?"

"Kind of. Most of the time, he's not around and we like it that way. I think you can see why. But you're lucky. I know everyone in your new department and I can assure you. You don't have a Keith over there." I laugh again.

"You said the company has a future. What did you mean?" he asks.

"Well, Empire, Inc. has a great product line. We could double our profits if they would just change their mindset."

"Explain what you mean." Taylor seems really interested.

"Management is old fashioned. I made a couple of presentations. I thought the sales department was going to suffer a collective heart attack when I mentioned focusing on a new demographic, ages eighteen through twenty-five. After that, it was like they all went deaf simultaneously, didn't hear anything else I said. They're not open to new ideas. We're a successful company, make good enough profits for our shareholders. They're just afraid to try something new."

"Then why have you stayed with the company so long?"

"Well, it wasn't my life plan. I intended to stay two, three years, get some experience and then head for a big city; New York or Chicago. But my dad had a stroke, and wasn't able to work anymore. I couldn't leave my mom alone with my two younger siblings. She's a schoolteacher, and they don't make much. A little money comes in from my dad's pension, but I had a good, steady job. Before long, my younger sister got married. My brother is a sophomore in college. So, it will be a couple of years before I can leave Empire, if I even want to. Maybe Loretta and I will go to Europe then," I laugh.

"Hey everybody, look at Nona hitting on the new hire!" Keith yells. "Hey Nona, are you hitting on our new employee?"

"No, Keith, I am not hitting on our new employee, but if you'll come over here, I'd be happy to hit *you,*" I retort. All of my friends howl, even Taylor.

Of course, Keith doesn't think it's funny.

"I'm going to report you to H.R. first thing Monday morning, Nona. You threatened me with physical violence and I have witnesses," Keith says.

Taylor speaks up. "I didn't hear Nona threaten Keith. Did anyone else hear her threaten him?"

Everyone at the table answers in unison, "No, we didn't hear anyone threaten Keith."

Keith's face is beet red and he shouts down the table, "Screw you Taylor! You don't know who you're dealing with."

"That's it." Taylor says. "Walter, would you agree that Keith has had too much to drink?"

"Yeah, I guess so." Walter looks confused.

"Did Keith drive here or was he a passenger in someone else's car?" Taylor asks.

"He drove with me," Nate answers.

"Okay Nate, you're gonna have to call a cab for Keith. He's gonna be leaving now," Taylor says with authority.

Swiveling to face Keith, Taylor says, "Keith, you're going home. Make sure you leave enough cash to pay for your food."

Loretta leans behind Taylor, looks at me and mouths: "Superhero."

"I'm not leaving. I haven't even finished my dinner," Keith states forcefully.

"Keith, look at me. You are going home now. I don't care if you've finished your food or not," Taylor says with a tone of voice that leaves no room for argument.

"Can I get a doggie bag?" Keith asks.

"No, Keith, just go," Taylor says emphatically, and I feel the hairs on the back of my neck stand up. We sit in silence as Keith gets up and slowly walks out of the restaurant.

Taylor turns back to me, smiles and says, "I'd love to see those presentations you talked about."

"I'll have to get Peter's permission, but I'd gladly show them to you. You might have better luck than me." I say shrugging my shoulders.

"Since I'm a man, you mean," Taylor says. "I understand that Peter won't be there Monday."

"Really? He usually lets me know if he's taking a day off."

Taylor waves a waiter over and orders three bottles of their best champagne. We are all in a much better mood now that Keith is gone.

Taylor uncorks the champagne like a pro, and when all the glasses are poured, he stands and says to everyone, "I have an announcement to make. I was busy this morning buying a new company. So, I won't be your new coworker because I'm actually your new boss. I just bought Empire, Inc."

We're all in shock. Taylor sits back down next to me, smiling, and says, "I have to make a confession. You see, I've already reviewed your two presentations, and I loved all of your ideas. I have great plans for the company and I have great plans for you, too. I think together, we can build Empire into a new, modern company that could more than double in size within a year. What do you say? Are you ready to take a chance?"

Before I can answer, another waiter appears with a tray piled high with ice cream to go with my birthday cake, compliments of Tony's.

Jordon

I SEE HER IN THE FOYER AND FOR A SECOND, MY HEART STOPS. I STAND UP so she can see where I'm seated, and she heads my way. She's wearing dark brown leggings, a long beige sweater with a big collar and brown suede, high heel boots. She's a tall woman and as slim as I remembered. I know that even now, I could pick her out of a large crowd. I also know that I still love her.

I smile and indicate the seat across from me, wait until she sits, and I say, "I'm so glad you came. I was afraid you might not show."

We sit examining each other closely. She now wears her mass of auburn hair longer, and her green eyes look tired. Her only jewelry is a pair of large, gold earrings and—unfortunately—a wide, gold wedding band.

After a pause she says, "I almost didn't."

"Well, I'm glad you did. You look amazing. You haven't changed at all." I smile.

"Don't start out by lying to me. It's been almost ten years," she answers, and I know I've annoyed her.

"Well, I see a few gray hairs and more laugh lines around your eyes, but you still look beautiful to me." I really mean it.

"Don't go there," she snaps.

"Okay, okay."

"You look better, healthier than the last time I saw you," she says.

"Well, I've been sober for the last seven years, I *should* look better," I laugh.

She smiles.

The waiter comes and takes our drink orders.

"Black decaf coffee for me, and what would you like, Faith?"

"Coffee's fine."

"That's not necessary. Do you still drink Chardonnay?" I raise my eyebrows.

"If you're sure that's okay, I'd like that," she answers politely.

"Please bring the lady your best Chardonnay."

The waiter nods and hands us each a menu.

"At the hotel, they said this was a pretty popular place. Have you ever been here?" I ask without looking up.

"Yes, the food here is excellent. If you're still into Italian, they have the best in town. They also have great French choices and the standard steak and potatoes. I've never heard anybody complain about their food," she says from behind the menu.

"Do you come here often?" Oh God, what a dumb thing to say. It sounds like an old pick-up line.

"No, only on special occasions." She puts her menu down on the table.

We both order a Caesar salad, then I order the large serving of lasagna with extra bread. Faith picks some French chicken thing that comes with a cream sauce on top. I dig into my salad. I'm starving since I haven't eaten all day. I've been too nervous.

"Why are you here, Jordon?" Faith asks.

I almost choke on my lettuce. I was hoping we could enjoy our meal first, but Faith always has been very direct.

"Well, you've heard of the Twelve Step Program—Alcoholics Anonymous? Well, Step Nine is all about making amends to those that you've hurt, and you are the last person on my list. I've come to tell you how very sorry I am for hurting you, Faith," I say, as sincerely as possible.

"And it took you almost ten years to get around to me?" Faith sits absolutely still.

Jesus, now my stomach is in knots. I'll never be able to eat. Why couldn't she have waited another hour before we got into this?

"I know I hurt you more than anyone else." I can feel the muscles in my throat tightening. "I knew this would be the hardest conversation I had to have. I know I can never make amends for what I did to you."

Tears start in Faith's eyes. She takes her napkin, wipes them dry and says, "Never mind. I forgave you years ago. Let's eat." And with that, she picks up a fork full of lettuce and she continues to consume her salad.

To say I am stunned is an understatement. I know she's lying, and now I'm getting mad. She has every right to be furious with me. And now she has made me feel invisible, unimportant, and inconsequential. Suddenly, I almost want to laugh. Bravo, Faith, the perfect revenge.

"How is she?" I ask.

"She's great. She's just finishing fifth grade, getting great grades. She's really smart." She smiles.

"Does she remember me?"

"Nope, she was just a toddler. It's a blessing, don't you think?" She continues eating.

Another point for you, Faith.

"Where did you go? I looked everywhere for you when I got out of rehab. I couldn't find you. No one would tell me where you'd gone." I try not to sound agitated.

"I swore everyone to secrecy. I was finished with you, Jordon. I wanted to start over. I didn't need you showing up, spoiling my new life. Let's just eat. Talk about where we are now, not the past. What do you do now?" Faith shows no emotion, she remains absolutely still. She doesn't fidget like she used to.

"It was rough at first," I say and take a sip of my coffee. "But I finally decided to go back to school and finish my degree. I only needed one more semester. There was a notice in the cafeteria one day calling for volunteers to work on a project for Habitat for Humanity that weekend. I'd never done anything like that and thought I'd give it a try."

I'm leaning my elbows on the table while I talk, using my fork to emphasize certain words. I want to impress Faith with my sincerity. I can't believe my appetite is coming back, but the lasagna is delicious.

"Most of the others goofed off," I continue, "but a few of us really got into it. I struck up a conversation with the owner of the construction company that was building the houses and I kept volunteering every weekend. I asked so many questions and caught on so quickly that when I graduated, he offered me a job, not only working on houses, but also managing the office. I've never done anything I loved so much. I've been there seven years. The company has expanded so fast, I'm now their new vice president."

"I'm really happy for you, Jordon." She smiles, but it doesn't reach her eyes.

"What about you?" I ask nervously. "Where did you go? What did you do?"

"Well, you know my parents disowned me when I got pregnant, so my Aunt Theresa, who lives in San Antonio, offered to help. We moved there, and she babysat Patty while I went back to school, too. I finally finished nursing school, even got my R.N. That way I could make a decent living for the two of us, no matter where we lived. I worked in Texas for about a year, but it was way too hot for me, so we moved to Colorado. I liked colder weather and the season changes. We ended up in Vail." She smiles and tosses her head to the side as if that's the end of her story.

"How did you end up here?" I ask her.

"That's a long story," she says, and it's obvious she's finished talking.

"I noticed your wedding ring. So, you're married now. Is that part of the story?" I smile.

"No. Well—yes. I'm a widow. I met Tom in Vail. He was up there on a ski trip. He had a pretty serious accident, fractured his leg in several places. He was facing a longer stay in the hospital and weeks of rehab. I was doing independent work at the time, and he hired me as his full-time private nurse for as long as he had to stay in Colorado. He was older than me," she explains.

"You seem to be drawn to older men, Faith. Heck, I was already out of the Marines when we first met."

"You're not that much older than me—what, six years? I thought, because you were a vet, you were more mature. You were nothing like the other guys in college. You had a goal. You were working toward a degree in finance so you could take over your father's business. You had us all fooled, Jordon, even your parents." There is a touch of venom in her voice.

"I also had a lot of baggage, Faith," I try to explain.

"Never mind. Do you want to hear my story or not?" she asks, and she's angry now.

"Sorry, I didn't mean to get into all that."

"Tom was quite charming and the perfect patient. We really hit it off. Once he was ready to head back home, he asked for my personal phone number. I'd never given that number to a patient before, but I figured I'd never see him again. Well, it turned out Tom owned a very successful company and was quite wealthy. He ended up calling me every day just to check in, ask how I was doing. He thought nothing of hopping on a plane if I had the weekend off so we could go out to dinner or catch a movie."

Faith takes a sip of her wine.

"I'd say Tom swept me off my feet, but I loved every minute of it. Patty loved him as much as I did. We had a house in New York and one here in town. This is where Tom was born. The three of us had five wonderful years together. Tom passed away eight months ago, a heart attack. He left us well taken care of. I never have to worry about Patty's future ever again. Patty and I both loved it here so much, we decided to live here permanently."

Faith stops speaking, but I can see the pain in her eyes. It's ridiculous to envy a dead man, but I do. How I wish I could have made Faith as happy as Tom did.

"I'm sorry things didn't work out for you. He sounds like a great guy," I admit.

"He was. We were blessed to have him for as long as we did." She smiles.

"I want to meet her, Faith."

"No, absolutely not." Faith is adamant.

"Faith, don't be like that. I've been sober all this time. I think I've earned the right to see her, to get to know her."

"You haven't earned the right to anything. Ten years ago, you went into rehab. That facility cost your family a fortune, and I thought you'd come out of there and put your life back together. But what did you do? In less than a year, you were right back where you started. And for almost three years, you were in and out of rehab."

Faith doesn't even raise her voice. She doesn't even care enough to be angry at me. I don't remember her being this cold.

"Yeah, I had a tough time until my dad finally talked me into checking myself into the V.A. hospital," I say. "I got professional counseling there. The Alcoholics Anonymous group I told you about—we're all vets. I still go to those meetings. There's a lot of stuff that went on over there in Afghanistan that us guys have had trouble processing. A lot of us have nightmares. You remember the nightmares, don't you?"

"Well, I'm really glad you finally got your head on straight. But I still don't trust you enough to allow you into Patty's life. After all, you say you've been sober seven years and you just now got around to wanting to see your daughter? She hasn't crossed your mind in all this time?" Faith asks sarcastically.

"That's not true. My mom helped me hire a private detective to look for you as soon as I got sober. He finally found your address last week. The minute he called my mom's house with the news, I booked a flight here. In reality, I've been looking for you for the last ten years."

"Why didn't *she* just tell you where I was? I've kept in touch with your parents all along. They had a right to know what happened to their granddaughter. I've written to them, sent them pictures." Faith's voice is defensive now.

"You mean my mother has known where you were all this time?" I slam my fist down on the table, and I'm pleased when the ice princess jumps.

"Yes," she says in a whisper.

"Why would she keep this from me? I bet she never even hired an investigator."

I have to calm down. I'll deal with my mother later.

"In the beginning, probably because you were still drinking, and then because I begged her not to let you know where I was. Once you got sober, I'm sure she didn't know how long you would stay that way. By the time she was convinced it was permanent, I was married to Tom. She probably didn't want you interfering with my life. And I thank her for that," Faith states firmly.

"Well, I don't. Now that you know the truth, will you give me a second chance, and at least let me meet my daughter?"

"I don't know. I'll have to think about it. But you better not hurt her. She's all I have," Faith says, tears forming in her eyes.

"That's not true, Faith. You're not alone. Not at all! Please, come home for Thanksgiving. Let Patty meet her grandparents, her aunts, her uncles, her cousins, and, just maybe, her dad."

Martha

I REQUEST A TABLE BY THE WINDOW, SIT DOWN AND ORDER A GLASS OF white wine. I'm glad I didn't check my jacket since I'm still chilled from the evening air. I sip my drink and browse through the menu. It's a small, pricey, elegant restaurant; the kind you find sprinkled throughout most metropolitan cities. Soft music plays in the background, not quite elevator music, but close. The décor is cool greens, dark paneling, with lots of plants, linen tablecloths, sterling silverware, and crystal. I'm in no hurry, have lots of time and no place to go.

Lightning brightens the sky, and thunder rumbles in the distance. Well, rain was in the forecast. What shall I eat? Everything looks enticing.

I'm drawn to the couple the minute they enter the foyer. First, I notice how young they are—early thirties, perhaps. They look happy, even excited. He's tall, handsome, well over six-foot, dark hair, dark eyes, Mediterranean, perhaps. She's also tall, trim, with what I like to call California hair, sun-streaked blond. They look successful. His navy blue suit is tailor made; her red wool dress seems expensive. She's carrying a Gucci purse.

I wonder if they work together. Are they celebrating a promotion? Could this be a first date? No, they are far too comfortable with each other. Leaning closer, he puts his arm around her shoulders.

I decide on the shrimp and place my order. I nurse my wine and watch the reflection of the candle on my table dancing in the window.

The thunder grows louder, closer and it's starting to sprinkle outside.

I find the couple a few tables off to my left. He's speaking, leaning forward. She's gazing at him with that look of pure adoration the young have perfected. They're too inexperienced to be jaded. He takes her hand and caresses her palm with his thumb. At one point, he raises her hand to his lips and kisses her fingertips. Definitely lovers.

I'm an older woman now, but not so old that I can't remember a lover's touch, the feel of his lips on mine, the anticipation of the night ahead. He makes a toast and I see the flash of wedding rings. Ah, they're married. I choose to believe they are married to each other. I've seen the heartbreak and destruction infidelity can cause, and, after all, this is my fantasy.

Tony's came highly recommended by the hotel concierge, and now I understand why. The shrimp is excellent: plump, juicy, not overcooked, just the right combination of butter and herbs. The rice is spicy, light and fluffy. I stop to butter my roll and look back at the couple.

It's her turn now. She is far more animated, talking with her hands, tilting her head left and right. She moves around in her seat, exuding energy. He watches her with a smile on his face, as if she is the only woman in the world. She's made him laugh. He has a nice laugh.

As I continue my meal, I wonder if they have children. I hope so. I've raised a family and know the joys, the heartaches but, oh, the rewards. Perhaps tonight is a night out without the kids; those few free hours to rediscover that you are more than just parents. First and foremost, you are lovers, and if you forget that, your marriage could be doomed.

Should I have dessert? It's raining much harder now, the trees are being tossed around by the wind. That makes up my mind. I order cheesecake and a pot of tea. I realize how tired I am; my feet hurt. I'll be glad to get back to my hotel room, lock in for the night and rest. I wonder if the couple will have dessert. No, I think not. By now they are probably anxious to be on their way, to be alone.

I contemplate the wonders of youth and ask myself what I miss the most. The answer is easy: it's you, Daniel. Loving you, the sound of your voice, your kindness, the way you always made me laugh. Forty years together and yet I feel cheated. I wanted more, much more. I miss you so much.

I'm not looking forward to tomorrow. I'm afraid the board of directors made a huge mistake when they said I could bring Harold to the meeting. I'm sure they felt the old lady could use an old friend, her lawyer, to convince her to sell her stock. I suppose they hope they can talk him into selling his holdings as well. They'll probably try to convince us they need our shares to help avoid the anonymous takeover that's threatening the company.

I remember the night you insisted I send for Hal. You were so ill. But the three of us had been dear friends since college, so I thought you just wanted to say good-bye. But when we entered the bedroom, there you were, sitting up, surrounded by papers and two booklets.

You said, "Listen to everything I say, and don't interrupt me."

You laid out what you believed the board of directors would attempt to do once you were gone: buying up outstanding stock, trying to pressure me and Hal into selling our shares, and then going after the children. You outlined their plan to take over the company and then sell it off to our largest competitor. At first, we thought you were delusional, imagining things. But then you showed us the paperwork for the firm you had established in Hal and my names. An anonymous corporation that was already busy buying up available stock, preparing for what you believed would come. You said you weren't sure when it would happen, but you knew it would come to pass.

I have to admit, we humored you that night. But still, knowing you, we remained vigilant.

Since everything was quiet for over two years, I was surprised when last year, they began to act. The board must have been shocked when they realized how few shares were available on the open market. Now they face a real takeover, and tomorrow they're about to find out exactly who the real majority stockholders are.

Daniel, you would be so proud of James. He never wanted to join the family business. He wanted to make it on his own. But when Hal and I contacted him about what the board was up to, he was all in. He confessed that a few of the foremen in the shop, the ones he worked for while he was in college, had contacted him about some of the changes being made at the plant. They've been purchasing cheaper parts for the machinery. Switching long-time contracts with quality companies to poorer quality outfits in China. The employees are afraid our product line is going to be affected. In fact, he was just about to come to me when we called him. He is going to take over management of the company, just as you always wanted our son to do.

Now, let's talk about Hal. That old fool confessed he has been in love with me ever since we were in college, and that you knew all along. He has proposed—asked me to marry him. He says he talked with you about his plans to ask me, before you passed. And that you gave him your blessing, and that you said the two of us could finally take all those trips we tried to get you to take.

It brought back such vivid memories, Daniel! Hal and I on our living room floor, surrounded by travel brochures for exotic trips to all those wonderful places: London, Paris, Italy, Egypt, safaris in Africa. All the places the three of us talked about visiting when we were college students. But no matter how short a trip we planned,—a quick flight, a short cruise—or how hard we tried to talk you into it, you always put the business first.

No matter how disappointed we were, you always said the same thing: "We'll have plenty of time for that when we retire."

But, sadly, you never did retire. How I wish you would have given in, just once.

Hal said we're both young enough to enjoy old age together, and we have something in common: we both loved you. He said we could honeymoon on one of those cruises I always wanted to take.

Well, it would have been nice if you had warned me so it wouldn't have been such a shock. I never did appreciate it when you tried to be controlling, Daniel. We had some major arguments about that tendency of yours. And I certainly don't appreciate you making plans for my future now that you're gone. Of course, Hal said you told him I'd feel this way. Oh well, let's just hope Hal and I can pull everything off tomorrow and save the company.

The first taste of cheesecake is sinful. Smooth and creamy on my tongue, with just a hint of lemon. It certainly exceeds expectations. I understand the five-star reputation.

I check on the couple again. I wish I could cross the room, join them, impart some words of great wisdom. But what would I say?

Cherish each touch, every moment. It goes by so fast. One morning you wake up, look in the mirror and you're old. And then you wonder, when did that happen?

I smile. They wouldn't listen, wouldn't understand—the young never do.

They are leaving now. He helps her with her coat, gives her a quick hug and whispers in her ear. At the front door, he pulls her collar up around her neck and buttons the top button against the cold. They run past my window, arms around each other, heads bent into the wind, and they appear to be laughing.

I check my watch. Hal had business in California tonight and is flying in on the red eye. His plane won't land until after midnight, and then he'll have to drive all the way from the airport. I won't see him until early tomorrow morning, at breakfast. I wonder if he is as nervous as I am about the meeting. I doubt it. After all, Hal ran a very successful law firm for almost thirty years. He probably can't wait to deal with the board. I'm sure he'll enjoy the looks on their faces when they realize they've been outmaneuvered, mostly thanks to you, Daniel.

After the big meeting, I have so many decisions to make. What will I say to Hal? Am I too old to get married again? Do I want to get married again? Would I be willing to live with Hal without getting married? Would Hal be shocked by such a notion? What am I going to tell the children? Should I discuss this with them beforehand? I think James would be happy for me. But what about the girls? They've known Uncle Hal their whole lives. Will they approve or disapprove?

I almost chuckle out loud at the vision of me telling them I might choose to live in sin. Frankly, at this point, do they even get a vote in how I live my life? As long as you approved, Daniel, shouldn't that be enough? And if I say yes, am I too old to have a wedding? Should it be a small affair, or should we just go to the Justice of the Peace?

So many questions. I have decided tonight I'll just do my Scarlett O'Hara impersonation and not worry about anything until tomorrow. I'll go back to my room, maybe rent a movie and go to bed early. I sip my tea and watch the rain run down the window. I wonder if Hal is definitely committed to a cruise or perhaps, at first, he'd consider just a couple of weeks in Paris.

Albert

"EXCUSE ME, SIR, BUT THE COUPLE AT THE TABLE BY THE WINDOW WOULD like me to ask you a question," says the young waiter.

"What kind of question?" I ask.

"Well, the gentleman noticed your cap when you came in and he wonders if you might be in town for the convention. The crowd in the restaurant tonight seems to be really picking up. They can see you standing in the foyer, and they know how cold it can get out here so they thought you might like to share their table."

"Do you know those people?" I ask my daughter.

She leans forward to get a better look. The couple at the table smiles and gives us a finger wave.

"Nope." Gale smiles. "But we were just about to leave, and I really would like us to spend at least one night at my favorite restaurant before you head back."

"Oh, well, what the hell. We can always leave if we don't enjoy their company," I laugh.

I watch the man observe us as we approach their table. He seems really interested in my brown cowboy boots peeking out from under my blue slacks. And as we draw closer, he seems to study Gale's eyes and mine, which are an almost identical bright blue.

The man rises and extends his hand. He is tall, approximately six feet, in his late fifties, with salt and pepper hair and light brown eyes. He is wearing brown slacks and a brown tweed sports jacket. His wife is a few years younger and has stylishly cut and professionally colored honey blond hair, green eyes and is wearing a kelly-green silk blouse and gray slacks, with a diamond pendant and diamond studs.

"Hi, my name is Troy Harrison and this is my wife, Claire," the man says.

"Pleased to meet you. My name is Albert Bryant, but my friends call me Al, and this is my daughter Gale."

Troy and I shake hands and then Gale and I take our seats. The waiter brings us our menus.

"I see by your hat that you're here for the big Vietnam veterans convention that's in town this weekend. Are you both from out of town, Al?"

"Just me. I'm from Texas. I hadn't intended to attend the convention this year, but when they decided to hold it here, I couldn't miss the chance to visit my daughter. She doesn't get back to Beaumont much."

"I live in that big, new development, Shady Oaks, just north of town," Gale says. "But I work downtown. So, it's been perfect. I can drop Dad off for all the events and pick him up whenever he's ready to go."

"I really hoped you would join us. I'm a history professor at a local college. I teach a whole quarter on the Vietnam War. I was at the convention just yesterday, and I attended a session where they showed new, never before seen, films about the Special Forces that served in the jungles in 'Nam in the early sixties. They were amazing." Troy really seems enthused.

"Yeah, I heard about that," I say.

"Were you there? Wasn't the presentation wonderful?"

"Well, I didn't go; I was too afraid I'd see myself on the screen." I laugh, but I'm not comfortable discussing the newly discovered films.

The four of us turn to our menus. Gale laughs and says, "I know what my dad will have. He loves lasagna, and it's great here, Dad."

We order our food and drinks. I get a Michelob Light. Troy asks if I'm retired.

"Oh, I retired about two years ago," I say. "Worked out at the refinery for about fifteen years, bought a garage with a friend of mine and started working on cars. We were both real handy and the business just grew and grew. Made a lot of money. Two years ago, we were both able to turn it over to our sons."

"And what about you, Gale?" Troy asks.

"I'm a lawyer. I work for Walker & Walker, Esq. They have offices at 2020 Main St." Gale answers.

"Yeah, the big skyscraper," Troy says with a smile. "I've been there. In fact, I know Mr. Walker Senior. He's on the board at the college."

"Are you both from here? Locals?" Gale asks kindly.

"No. We're both from Minnesota - cold country. Couldn't move further south fast enough. Do you like your job at the law firm, Gale?"

Teasingly, Claire says, "Al and Gale, you have to forgive Troy. He asks so many questions because I think he secretly wishes he had worked for the C.I.A. And he's always looking for information about the war to pass along to his students."

I laugh and say, "Well, we had plenty of those C.I.A. guys running around in 'Nam, that's for sure."

"Does your wife ever attend the conventions?" Troy asks.

"She used to. But I lost Winnie about three years ago."

"Oh, I'm so sorry. I shouldn't have brought it up."

"No, it's fine. We had a good life. A happy marriage." I look at Gale and we begin to chuckle. "Eventually."

"Eventually?"

"Well, here's a story I guess you could tell your class." I remove my reading glasses and begin to polish them.

"Winnie and I got married right out of high school. I was eighteen and she was seventeen. We were wed about four months, when I came home from work one Friday night and I told her I was going out drinking with the boys. Well, she informed me that I was now a married man. I couldn't just go out drinking with my friends like when I was single anymore. We had bills to pay."

I take a gulp of beer and continue. "We had a huge argument. I wasn't gonna let no woman tell me what to do. I stormed out of the apartment. Went out drinking anyway. I worked out at the refinery. That was hot and dirty work. I figured I deserved a night out. But I had a few too many. So, I tried to think what I could do to teach her a lesson."

I take another sip of beer and smile.

"I came up with this great idea. I was gonna just disappear, not tell anybody what I planned to do. I'd go and join the army. How's that for a plan? And that's just what I did. Now I was a strong, big ol' Texas boy, played football. Bootcamp was a snap.

"My sergeant said. 'Boy, I think you could make it as a Green Beret.'

"I puffed out my chest and answered, 'Yes, Sir.' And I damn near killed myself, but I got that beret. But, one day, I go to the quarter master to pick my pay and he said, 'Soldier, you somehow forgot to tell us about your sweet little wife back in Texas. You won't be getting a paycheck until we catch up with all her back benefits. We'll notify you when you'll be getting your next paycheck. And it will be quite a while before you hear from us.'

"So, there I was, walking around camp, not even able to afford a pack of cigarettes."

I laugh, shaking my head. Even after all these years, I can still laugh about what a fool I was.

"Then we start hearing rumors about a little problem in Southeast Asia. Talk about sending some Green Berets in as 'special advisors', whatever that meant. I went from the Gulf of Mexico to the Gulf of Tonkin in a flash."

I taste my lasagna and drink some ice water. I wonder if they want to hear the rest of my story, and everyone is still looking at me, so I continue.

"Eight of us were given a mission: go into the jungle and train the Vietnamese to fight the Viet Cong. The only problem was, these men weren't soldiers. We had several dozen rice farmers who had never even seen a gun and we were supposed to turn them into fighters. We had to give them weapons, teach them how to load, aim, shoot, break them down, clean and reassemble them. None of them spoke a word of English, and we only had two interpreters. They were great people. They loved their country and wanted to learn to fight for it."

I order another beer and ask Troy and Claire if they're getting tired of listening to me. But they shake their heads, apparently eager for me to continue.

"We taught them a lot about how to use guns and rifles, but try as we might, we never could teach them how to be quiet. They would march through the jungle talking and laughing. Sometimes at night, us G.I.s would get them settled down, and then we'd climb up and sleep in the trees because we were afraid the Viet Cong were gonna ambush us. We were convinced they had tracked us down due to all the noise." I chuckle.

"Were you ever attacked?" Troy asks. He and Claire seemed to be hanging on my every word.

"No but we did come pretty close two nights in a row. Viet Cong patrols passed by, about twenty feet away. That first morning, we had given them another lecture on how sound travels in the jungle and fortunately, they were extremely quiet both of those days. I guess our lectures had sunk in." I pause.

"Then every once in a while, one of the men would announce we were only a mile or two from his uncle or his brother's village. They would want to stop and visit their relatives. We always hated these impromptu stops, because we never knew if any Viet Cong spies were living in one of them or not. Whenever we arrived though, we were treated like heroes. The people wanted to prepare huge feasts and we knew they had so little. They would fix big pots of some kind of soup with chunks of unknown substances floating around. We never asked what it was, knowing it could be anything: goats, snakes, rats. You just accepted the gift and ate as little as possible." I laugh.

"But we always sent scouts out before we left, so we wouldn't walk into a trap. We'd already done that once and swore we'd never do it again. After being embedded for over a year, we had only lost one fellow Green Beret and one of our interpreters. Then, on the date we were finally to be extracted, they couldn't find us for over a week because our radios weren't working." I smile and shake my head.

"What happened when you got back to the States?" Claire asks.

"I had a bunch of back pay waiting, which was nice," I say with a laugh. "But the worse thing was, I had to face Winnie. She wasn't one bit happy to see me. The eighteen-year-old immature kid she married was replaced by a twenty-one-year-old, battle-weary Green Beret."

I take a gulp of beer before continuing.

"I think the only thing that saved me was, after all that time in the jungle, I was just skin and bones. I had injured my ankle and walked with a limp. She finally did forgive me, but she made me work for it." I smile big, remembering those years, and say, "I really taught her a lesson, didn't I?"

We all laugh so loud that we attract some attention.

Claire asks if anyone would like dessert, adding that Tony's has wonderful chocolate cake and rice pudding.

Gale almost spits coffee across the table. She looks at me and we both begin to laugh.

"What's so funny?" asks Troy.

"I ate rice damn near every day, for every meal, almost seven days a week, the whole time I was in the jungle. We were always running out of our K-rations and the Vietnamese we were training always carried plenty of rice. They ate it at every meal and were always willing to share. When we were in those villages, the soup was served over mounds of rice. I swore if I ever made it out of there alive, I'd never eat another grain of rice for the rest of my days, and so far, I've kept my promise. So, if it's okay with you, I'll stick to chocolate cake."

As the meal draws to a close, I take out my credit card, but Troy holds up his hand and says, "This is on me. You've given me an awesome story to tell my students. It's been a great pleasure. The next time you're in town, Al, I hope you'll call us. I'd love for you to come and talk to my students, tell them some more stories about the war."

"I really don't like to talk much about the war. Most of my memories aren't very happy ones. Buddies from my neighborhood who didn't make it home, or came back and never were the same. And then the way it ended. I didn't mind sharing the one about what a dumb-ass kid I was, though," I laugh.

We all stand, and Troy and I shake hands. The women say their goodbyes before I grab Gale's arm and head for the door.

I hate long goodbyes.

Kelly

OH GOD, I HATE SATURDAY NIGHTS.

It can get so hectic here. Someone always calls in sick, and we have to cover their tables. This is the third time Frankie hasn't shown up, and she didn't even call. I really like her, but now she may get fired. In the five months I've worked here, I've never stayed home on a Saturday night, but after tonight I may reconsider that practice.

I've always worked in restaurants much larger than Tony's with a faster turn-over. This place is smaller; the tables are much closer together. We have to dance around like ballerinas, balancing heavy trays on our shoulders while staying invisible. It's a posh place, high prices with rich clientele. But if you think rich equates to big tips, think again. How can people with so much give so little? When I make it, I'll be different. I'll be a big tipper. After all, I know firsthand how hard it is to wait tables. Oh well, at least no one here has patted me on the ass so far.

Thanks to the high prices, we make pretty good money here. I don't mind hard work; in fact, I wish we could speed things up a bit. It's the kind of place where customers come to celebrate—graduations, anniversaries, baby showers—so they talk, laugh and just linger. We had a party here earlier this evening. They certainly had a good time. Cake, champagne, everybody singing Happy Birthday off-key. Fortunately, none of the tables around them complained. Everyone seems to be in a good mood tonight.

But the music doesn't help. If the owner tried something with a beat, maybe people would eat and drink faster. The more tables you serve, the more money you make. In addition, eight hours of this music starts to get on my nerves. I like my music faster and with words, thank you. But then, with that I might be tempted to *really* dance around the tables.

They keep the temperature in here comfortable for the diners. However, hustling tables is hot work. It's cold and rainy outside tonight, lots of thunder and lightning. If you're by the front door when it's opened, you get blasted with cold, damp air. Then you go in the kitchen and hit that wall of heat and humidity. It's the kind of atmosphere that makes the curls slide right off your head and your mascara run, if you're dumb enough to wear any. It's a wonder we don't all catch pneumonia.

The chef is a regular prima donna, expecting us to pick up the food the minute it's plated. He acts as though we have nothing better to do than stand around waiting for his masterpieces. And God forbid you bring something back. It's not *my* steak that isn't well done enough or *my* soup that is too spicy. Then he looks ready to kill the messenger. And he's always yelling at the kitchen help. I'm glad I don't work in there with those poor guys. I'd likely get fired because, with my temper, I'd just yell right back at him.

In addition to being hectic, Saturday is couples' night. Everywhere you look, happy couples are enjoying a night out. God, I wish I was part of a couple again. But not until I get my degree. Thanks to my job here at Tony's and the fact that we're not open for lunch, I've been able to take three early morning classes this semester instead of just one night class. So, I don't mind putting my dating life on hold. It's not that I haven't had plenty of opportunities. Guys at work and guys at school have asked me out. But they just don't fit into my plans right now. I need a guy who understands how important getting my degree is to me. One who would be supportive, not get mad if I couldn't go out because I have to study. Too many guys are needy; they want to be the center of attention. Like our bartender Nick. He's a nice enough guy. He asks me out almost every night. He just won't take "no" for an answer. He's convinced I'm playing hard to get. When I tell him I have to study for a test, he just rolls his eyes and acts like I'm lying.

One more year of school and I can probably get a job interning at a law firm. I don't want to be part of just any couple; I want to be one of these couples. I want the salon styled hairdo, expensive clothes, great perfume, a rock on my left hand big enough to ice skate on and the movie star husband. I want a guy who will look at me like the guy at table six looks at his wife. She's a lucky woman. He's a classy guy. Every time I bring their food or drinks, he looks right at me and says, "thank you." He doesn't act like I'm invisible.

On top of that, he is flat out gorgeous. Come to think of it, I want him. I want him in a big house in the suburbs, with a three-car garage and a new sports car. I want to work only if I feel like it; have a couple of kids, join the country club, play tennis and serve on a few charitable committees. I want the good life—the really, really good life.

Great, the guy at table four wants his check. He holds up his arm and snaps his finger like he's calling a dog. I wonder if he'll want me to roll over when I get there. I've seen it all – guys who wave their hands like they're holding a little flag; guys who whistle; women who call *"yoo-hoo!"* Not like table six. He just catches my eye and inclines his head. A classy guy.

Sunday nights are usually better. A few empty tables, but we still make good money. People seem to be in a hurry on Sundays; they don't hang around as much, so turnover is high. Maybe they're getting back into work mode, preparing for Monday. Except for tomorrow—that's the big DeMarco anniversary party. Louis said it's an "all-hands-on-deck" kind of affair. I didn't know what that meant at first, but someone said it's some kind of Navy expression. One of the waiters said Louis's dad was in the Navy.

The DeMarco family has rented out more than half of the restaurant. Seems they are long-time customers of the original restaurant, when Anthony's parents ran the place, so they deserve top drawer treatment. We have to come in two hours early. But Louis said the boss is paying us overtime and I can use the money. Anthony's a good man, and he always treats us fair.

And then comes Monday, glorious Monday. No work, no school, I can just soak in a hot tub and eat bon-bons. If only I could afford bon-bons. Of course, I always have to study. I never have much free time.

The only downer is, this Monday, I need to call my dad, check on how he's doing. I put it off last week. I was studying for a big test and couldn't face the lectures again. Why won't I come home, face my responsibilities, take care of Dale? His beloved son Dale, twenty-four years old and still not working. I've been taking care of him since I was twelve years old and my mom died.

It's not his fault that my parents spoiled him. He was born premature and was so tiny when they brought him home. I remember I thought he was one of my baby dolls. My mom would let me hold him and before long I was feeding him and changing his diapers. I was too young to realize that the fact that my mother's cough was getting worse and worse meant she had cancer and was gonna die. Poor Mom, she never believed what people told her about smoking. She and dad had been smoking since they were kids. The tobacco companies said cigarettes were safe. Even when they admitted they had lied, it was too late. She tried to quit several times, but never could. She kept telling me she was gonna be fine and there was nothing to worry about. She was going to get better real soon.

I was just a kid myself and I believed her. I knew she was sick, but I never thought she was gonna die. People never told children about really serious things back then. All I knew was my Mom was there one day and the next, she was gone. Everyone just told me she was with God in heaven and I was now the mother in the house. I needed to take care of Dale. He was eight years old by then and was a handful. Dad started drinking and was a constant problem. I woke Dad up every morning and yelled at him until he got up and got ready for work. I was so afraid he'd lose his job, and we'd have no money coming in. But I also kept after Dale. He wasn't a bad kid, never got in any trouble with the police. Thankfully, I caught him and his buddy Gerard the first time they tried marijuana. I think I scared the bejesus out of them because he never tried drugs again. It's just that Dad always depended on me and continued to spoil Dale.

Even through all the turmoil, I made sure Dale and I attended school. I always made time to study and kept my grades up high enough to get into college. I even went to my senior prom. My best friend, Lulu, said she had bought two dresses and couldn't decide between them. She asked me to come over and help her choose. Her mom and I both picked the beautiful rose-colored dress that looked amazing with her dark hair and eyes. Lulu's mom asked me to try on the other dress. It was a beautiful sky blue that matched my eyes. Her mom insisted I keep it and wear it to the prom. I was so thrilled that I cried, and it took me a few days to realize the dress was meant for me all along. I didn't have a date so I went with Lulu and her date. I'd never had that much fun before in my whole life.

Four years ago, I said I was finished. I told Dad he had to get his act together and sober up. I told Dale he had to grow up and get a job. They were both on their own, and I walked right out the front door. I try to call them once a week. But it's always the same old thing. Come home, I need you, Dale needs you.

I keep up with them through my friends, so I know Dad finally sobered up. He's fairly healthy and still working. He's even dating, which I find amazing. So, I'm kind of anxious to hear what sad tale he's gonna use to shame me into coming home this time. Maybe I'm wrong, maybe he'll tell me he's getting married; that he and his new wife are going to take care of Dale. Yeah, that's what he's going to say. Probably, he'll start nagging me about coming home for Thanksgiving and Christmas. I have an excuse for Thanksgiving: Tony's is open so I have to work. But I refuse to go home over Christmas break. In addition to a four-hour drive each way, spending three or four days in a house that reeks of cigarette smoke is more than I can bear. Besides, I have to study for my finals. And I can't handle the never-ending arguments with my dad about me coming home to take care of Dale. I'm sure Dale doesn't want me home any more than I want to come home.

Everything hurts—my feet, my legs, my back—and I have a headache. Gee, have I left anything out? I wish they had a place we could go lie down for about fifteen minutes, get off of our feet, relax and recharge. Maybe we should ask Anthony to install a cot in that back closet for when we are on a break. I'd like to see his face if we requested that in one of those group meetings that he calls every now and then. I have to get out of this business; I don't belong waitressing. But I'll wait tables until my feet fall off, as long as I get my degree and get a good job that pays real money. Until I can get a better life.

God, I hate Saturday nights.

Conway

"Why in the hell did he pick this place for the buy?" I ask, exasperated.

"Probably for the same reason we hate it. It's too small and way too crowded; he probably thinks he'll be safe here," Monroe answers.

"Hope this isn't another one of his tests; he better show." I respond. We've been working this case for a little over a year, and he's been playing games with us long enough.

Closing this case is really important to Monroe and me. Pedro Alvarez is a big-time cocaine dealer in the city, who also dabbles in the sale of heroin and meth. About six months ago, we got a tip that he's moving up in the organization. He's been importing fentanyl and synthetic opioids from Mexico. We've already worked several teenage opioid overdoses in our precinct alone. If we can finally make an arrest, maybe we can get him to give up his source. It may be a long shot, but it's what we're hoping.

I look across the table at Monroe and remember the day the captain called me into his office and told me my new partner was gonna be a woman. I wasn't too happy. I'm old school. Never wanted a partner I'd have to worry about, or someone I'd have to take care of. That first day she walked into the office, she's five foot, five inches tall, about one hundred and fifteen pounds, wearing blue jeans and a t-shirt. She looked about twelve. I already had twenty years' experience in drug enforcement. We all know it's dangerous work. I'm thinking, I'll be fighting my battles plus hers from now on. Boy, was I wrong.

I've seen her take down guys twice her size. In the academy, they teach that martial arts stuff. But like most men, I rely on brute force. Monroe took it one step further; she's a third-degree black belt. When she was on patrol, she arrested two six-feet-plus bikers all by herself. After she had them cuffed and in the patrol car, she asked, "Why didn't you fight me, considering my size?"

Looking at each other, one said, "Figured you were so small that if we gave you any trouble, you'd probably just shoot us."

She smiled and said, "You're probably right."

She likes to tell that one and she laughs a lot when she does. Monroe's okay. She's not very big, but well built—muscular. She wears her dark hair real short, almost a boy cut, claiming it's better for wearing wigs. She's a chameleon kind of woman. She can look like a seventeen-year-old waif or a twenty-year-old high-priced hooker, like she does tonight. She really doesn't fit in with the clientele here; she looks too brassy. But that's okay. Alvarez likes his women cheap and flashy.

Alvarez will search me for a wire, so I've mounted it and my radio under the table. They hid one on Monroe and she's trying to adjust it.

"I can't imagine where the hell they put that damn thing. If your skirt was any shorter, it would be a shirt," I say, rolling my eyes.

"I guess you'll just have to use your imagination." Monroe smiles and flutters her long, false eyelashes.

When she came into the squad room tonight, the team went nuts with whistling and catcalling. She just ignored them and, as we left, shot them the finger. Tonight, she's a blonde, wearing a skin-tight, red miniskirt with a low-cut red top and six-inch heels. She normally doesn't wear much makeup, certainly not this much, and I realize just how good-looking she is. Guess the single guys in the unit have already noticed.

Monroe and I have been working undercover, posing as representatives from an out-of-town drug dealer sent to negotiate a cocaine buy from Alvarez. As a result, we've had to spend blocks of time away from home, staying in a cheap hotel downtown. Alvarez picks places for a meet. Sometimes he shows and then sometimes he doesn't. So, we just have to wait.

"It's on the city's dime tonight so let's order something good," I say. "I'm gonna have a steak and a baked potato. How about you?"

"I think I'll just get the shrimp salad. I'm not that hungry." She usually doesn't eat much when we're undercover and she has to deal with a suspect like Alvarez.

We discuss everything but the case. We both know what we need to do. For now, we'll just relax. It wasn't always like this between Monroe and me. We weren't always this comfortable. In the beginning, she was reluctant to get too close. I doubt many in the department know that much about her private life, even now. She and her mom are from Chicago. They were both raising Monroe's three younger brothers there. The oldest of the three boys got mixed up in a gang and while Monroe was a rookie with the police department, she showed up at a crime scene and found him dead from a drug overdose. It almost broke her mom. Monroe worked the streets five years before she could get assigned to drug enforcement. After three years working there, she and her mother decided to relocate here. Due to her experience with the Chicago P.D., she was able to transfer right into Narcotics here.

Monroe bought a small house here in an upscale neighborhood, enrolled her youngest brother, Jamie, in a good middle school and her other brother, Jason, in an equally good high school. She is really involved in their lives, attending as many of their school activities as possible. She's determined to keep them out of trouble, away from any gang activity and drugs. Several times we've checked off-duty just to catch the end of one of the boys' football or baseball games. She has their friends over to the house frequently so she can check them out. Just like my wife and I did with our kids. Like Monroe said, she'd rather they were hanging out at her house than on a street corner.

"So, are you still dating that lawyer guy?" I ask.

"No, he was a jerk, just like you warned me," she laughs. "Am I wrong? I don't want to marry someone on the job. I see cops marry other cops, and it causes all kinds of problems." Monroe puts her elbow on the table and puts her chin in her hand.

"Cops have one of the highest divorce rates, profession-wise," I say. "You know that. It's not easy being married to a cop. It's a dangerous job and our hours are so erratic. It's hard for a spouse to handle that, and Narcotics is even worse."

"But you and Betty are happy."

"Yeah, but I married a saint," I smile. "Don't give up. You're young yet. You'll find somebody. I'll even help."

"Tell my mother I'm still young. And forget about helping me. That's all I need, you messing around in my personal life. Bad enough I have to work with you." She laughs.

She's just kidding. Betty and I have Monroe and her family over to the house frequently. We swap holidays. The Monroes take Thanksgiving one year and we take it next, same with Christmas.

"By the way," I say, "you do remember, Thanksgiving is at our house this year and it's just a few weeks away. Betty is already planning the menu."

"Oh, I know. My mom is gonna make tamales, same as usual. And I did meet this new guy…" Monroe trails off, then whispers, "It's show time." Her whole body language changes. She arches her back, tilts her head; damn, she's good.

Alvarez walks in, avoids eye contact with us, and gazes around the room, checking out each table. He's obviously made reservations because his two bodyguards are being seated at a table by the door. He's wearing an Armani navy blue pinstripe suit, lots of gold jewelry, and is carrying a briefcase that matches mine.

When he joins us, he's mesmerized by Monroe's cleavage and pays little attention to me. It's been a long year, and I'm ready to close this case. I can't imagine what Monroe is thinking as Alvarez's hand starts roaming up and down her arm.

"Hey sweetie, why aren't you eating? Do I have to send that back?" Alvarez asks Monroe.

"No, I'm just watching my figure," she answers coyly.

"So am I," he says with a smile. Sleazy bastard.

His hand is under the table now. I visualize it roaming up and down her leg and want to head for the men's room so I can throw up. How the hell does she do it? She must want to reach under there and break his wrist. I know I do.

I have to look away. Why the hell do we stay in Narcotics? Monroe and I have discussed it and our reasons are very similar. She still has nightmares of finding her brother's body, dead in an alleyway, when she didn't even know he was messing with drugs. She is dedicated to keeping drugs out of the hands of young kids. She hates to see parents go through what her mother endured.

In all the years I've been doing this job, it's the many additional lives I've seen destroyed by drugs. Not only the victims, most of them dead in their teens, but the parents and siblings. Lives that are never the same due to the loss of a loved one. Added to that, we're good at it. We've closed so many cases since we've partnered up, we lead the squad in convictions. But I have to be honest, it's also got to be the high—the adrenaline kick we experience when we slap the cuffs on, close the case, and get another dirtbag off the streets. Even knowing we'll never catch them all. There's always some other dirtbag waiting to take their place.

Betty would love this place. It's really fancy, wood paneling, dark green painted walls, brass lighting. We'll be married twenty-five years next month, so maybe I'll splurge and take her here for our anniversary. We were just kids when we got married. I had just graduated from the academy. I wasn't sure how she would handle being married to a cop. I heard all the stories about how cops always had a girlfriend on the side and all about the divorce rate. We talked about the hours and how I wanted us to be different. I wanted us to be the exception, the police couple who stayed together forever. Little did I know, Betty would take me seriously. Every anniversary she orders a cake that says, "Happy Anniversary, My Darling Exception." I expect I'll get one next month, too. God, I love that woman.

I'm ready to finally go back home, be with her and the kids. The twins are both still home. They're seniors in high school. The next-oldest is graduating from college in June, and the two oldest are both married. I know Monroe probably can't wait to get home and take a long hot shower to wash the scumbag's handprints off her body. He either has the drugs or he doesn't. And we're ready to nail this bastard.

I've got to get this thing moving. I start to fidget, act annoyed and say, "It's time to close this deal. Alvarez, let's get this show on the road."

We head for the men's room together just like a couple of girls. I check each stall; he pats me down. Alvarez doesn't have much to say, he's all business now. I test the stuff. It's first rate. We've got a deal.

Back at the table, we exchange briefcases. He leans over, hands Monroe a piece of paper and whispers in her ear.

She smiles and says, "Sounds good. I'll meet you there."

He leaves, followed by his two goons.

"What was that all about?" I ask as I throw a roll of money on the table to cover the tab, then grab my recorder and radio from underneath the table before we head out the door.

"I have a date tonight," Monroe laughs as we rush down the street. "That's his room number at the hotel where he's staying."

"You'll have to drop by his cell tonight and say hi. After we finish this, I want to hear about this new guy. Are you bringing him to Thanksgiving?"

I key my radio and shout, "Take them down; take them down. But don't cuff them yet."

Monroe looks at me, confused.

"This is Monroe's collar, guys," I call into the microphone, grinning. "She earned it."

Jennifer

Luckily, a table as far away from them as possible is available. I duck behind my menu and order God knows what to drink. I needn't worry; they haven't noticed me. They are totally absorbed in each other. They look like an average married couple, except he's much older than her. But I know differently. I know the truth.

You casually reach across the table and tuck her hair behind her ear. My hand flies to my own ear and imitates the gesture I know so well. How many times have you done that to me? We were married when I was so young. I was a freshman in college when we met. You were a junior. My parents weren't happy about our marriage. I dropped out of school with plans to work until you graduated. You promised when you got your degree, I could go back to school and get mine.

But after your bachelor's, you decided you needed your master's. And after graduation, you said it was time we started a family. After all, I wasn't getting any younger. Right after Amy was born, you announced you had accepted a new job in Denver, five hundred miles away from my family and all of our friends. Ever the supportive wife, I set about building us a new life. Your new job required lots of overtime, but I was content and we became well established in the community. Seven years later, you had accepted another new job, and we were on the move again. After all those years, I believed we had finally put down roots and our life there was permanent.

I have to order something if I intend to stay. Perhaps a fancy appetizer, the kind you always say are too expensive. It certainly won't be a salad. Who cares if I get fat now? All those years of dieting and exercise, for nothing.

I gaze around the restaurant. I've always wanted to come here. It's a beautiful place, but you always said our funds were too tight. Now I know why.

You are oh-so-charming and handsome. You always exercised, kept in shape, stayed heart healthy for the sake of our family. What an ass. You still have great hair, nice and thick. What a trick nature plays on us women. Men look so distinguished with their gray hair and we look so washed out. How I wish you had gone bald, like your dad.

Your deep blue, lying eyes look so sincere as you gaze at her. She stares at you, mesmerized. I felt that way more times than I care to remember. All your stories are brand new to her. Is that what you miss? A new audience to impress with your college football glory days, your war stories?

I expected her to be tall, slim, beautiful, something outstanding. Oh, she's pretty enough, and of course, she's a blonde, but nothing special. She's even chunky. She's wearing a navy blue pantsuit, no accessories, and in fact, her outfit is rather bland. Of course, she's almost young enough to be your daughter, give or take a few years. Is that what she has that I don't? Youth, no wrinkles or stretch marks.

I exercise, eat right, wash out the gray. I keep informed of national and world affairs, watch Oprah, read every *Cosmo* article on how to keep your man happy. I take care of you. I cook healthy, well-balanced meals, make sure you take your vitamins and that you keep your doctor's appointments.

Where did I go wrong? What could I have done differently? Is it me, or are you one of those men who are addicted to the chase? Or maybe I just didn't recognize a cheating bastard when one was standing right in front of me.

Last night, as I was up, pacing the floor, trying to decide what to do, I remembered that dinner party we attended at your obnoxious friend Gary's house. He decided to share his philosophy of why fidelity is so much easier for women than men. Since men are out in the business world exposed to so much temptation, he told us, it's harder for them to remain faithful. I watched you stand there, your head going up and down like a bobblehead doll, and thought you were just trying to be polite. I stole quick glances at the other women, who were staring off into space, and wondered if they, too, were remembering their own temptations.

I met Terry Walker the first year I was president of the P.T.A. He hung around after the first meeting to introduce himself. His daughter Carol and our daughter had become fast friends and he wanted to arrange a playdate. He started helping me put up the folding chairs and telling me a little about himself. He had grown up in Glenville, but had moved to Manhattan right after graduating law school. He had married. They started raising a family, one boy and one girl, while he was building his law practice.

His dream life was real, until four years ago, when his wife developed difficulty breathing. She was diagnosed with an aggressive form of lung cancer, even though she'd never smoked. By the end of the year, he was a widower, raising two small children in the middle of Manhattan. So, two years later, he packed up his kids and moved back home to be close to his parents. He had no regrets; Glenville, he said, is a great place to raise a family. All the chairs put away, we agreed to the playdate and Terry had volunteered to help with the elementary school Fall Festival. Terry was the kind of man who made me believe in reincarnation. After talking for an hour, I felt like I had known him my whole life.

Working on the festival was the happiest I had been in ages. Terry made me laugh, listened to my suggestions, and asked my opinions. He became my right-hand-man. He organized the fathers to help build the games for the festival, asked local businesses for donations, and even asked about you a few times. But when I always answered that you were working or out of town, he stopped asking. Of course, I soon realized I was becoming attracted to Terry and began feeling guilty. There you were, off working so hard, and I was enjoying the company of another man, even wishing deep down that I wasn't married. I knew I'd never act on those feelings. I loved you, and I would never break our wedding vows.

The festival was a huge success, and you did come to the wrap-up party. When I introduced you to Terry, you made an ass of yourself. I wondered if you could sense my attraction to him.

We were standing in a group when you said, "I guess it was really hard taking orders from a woman."

Terry just looked at you and said, "It depends on the woman. Jennifer is a born leader."

And then you followed up with, "I guess you took lots of orders from women in that big law firm you worked for in New York."

Terry smiled and answered, "Not exactly." And walked away.

I was so disgusted with you. I looked at you and in front of everyone, said, "Terry owned the law firm." Then I walked away.

When I caught up with Terry, I apologized for your behavior.

"I'm sorry," I said. "He's not usually like that. I don't know what got into him."

"No, I'm sorry," Terry said.

"What are *you* sorry about?" I asked.

"I'm sorry you're married to him. You deserve better. Goodbye, Jennifer."

I never saw Terry again. Two weeks later, you announced you had gotten another promotion and we were moving. I felt so guilty. I always suspected you knew how I felt about Terry. Last night I realized I should have paid more attention at Gary's party. You were agreeing that it was so hard for men to stay faithful because you never were faithful, and I was too dumb to realize it.

So, we packed up and moved again. The children and I had become accustomed to it by then. I researched the best neighborhoods and school districts to purchase a house, got the kids involved in after-school activities. Fortunately, the children take after their mom and both fit in easily. We made friends with other couples. I entertained your business associates. Once again, we became part of the community. But you've destroyed all of that now.

I'm almost dizzy with nausea. I shouldn't have come here. What was I thinking? I thought this would feed my anger, but all it's done is feed my pain.

They say deep down, the wife always knows when her husband is cheating, but I never suspected a thing. It took our twelve-year-old son to open my eyes. Whenever you work overtime, the kids and I make pancakes for dinner. We decorate them with chocolate chips, sprinkles and whip cream. When I mentioned last weekend that we should make pancakes on Sunday since you would be home for breakfast, Brian responded, "Mom, we eat pancakes all the time. Can't you make waffles?"

And that's when it hit me. What a fool I'd been to believe anyone could work that much overtime. That's when I decided to follow you tonight, still hoping I was wrong. Why didn't I stay home and keep pretending everything is okay? I thought I would be better off knowing the truth, but am I? Is there some way I can get out of here without being noticed? Does Tony's have another exit?

You take her hand and kiss the palm. My anger returns. How could you do this to us, to me? How long has she been in the picture? Is she the first? No, how many others? Do our friends know? Do they pity me or just laugh at me? How long have I been a fool? So many questions and only one solution.

I think about the gun in my purse.

Thanks to you, I am proficient with firearms. When we were first married, you insisted we spend all our weekends together. So, every fall, whenever you went hunting, you dragged me along, insisting I learn to shoot. Now, I appreciate that.

Who should I kill first? It will have to be you—you're stronger than I am, so I'll need to take you by surprise. Can I do this?

I suppose I shouldn't hate her as much as I do. She didn't break a vow to me or betray me, but I do. She could have resisted you. It's her fault. It has to be her, because I still love you.

I should just leave. Divorce you, take you for everything I can. But would it be enough? Could I handle the fact that you'd be off somewhere living a great life with her, not me? Plus, I would have to find a job and raise the children on my own while your life went on, maybe with a new family. No, I want more than that. I want you to suffer, to feel the pain I feel. To know real loss.

You get up to leave. She goes to the ladies' room and you take out your phone. When my cell phone rings, I almost fall off my chair. I frantically open my purse and find it.

"Hello."

"Hi Jen, it's me. I'm gonna be stuck here tonight, really late. We're working on a big proposal. I probably won't be home until after midnight."

How original. You sound so sincere.

"Where are you?" you ask. "I called the house first."

I want to scream, "Turn around, asshole!" Instead, I nervously answer, "I'm with Lisa. We decided to grab something quick to eat while the kids are at gymnastics." I hope my voice sounds normal.

"Okay then, don't wait up. And honey, kiss the kids goodnight for me."

Oh my God—my children. Have I lost my mind? Can I do this to them? Not only will I take away their father, but they'll have to face life knowing their mother was a murderer. Is it worth losing them just to get even with you? Are you worth it? What am I going to do?

Both of you hurry out the door, and I quickly signal for the check.

Miguel

¡POLICIA, POLICIA!

The word spreads through the kitchen like wildfire. My friends huddle in a corner, whispering. It isn't necessary; no one else in the kitchen speaks Spanish. It's fear—the belief that if they speak softly enough and are invisible enough, danger will somehow pass them by.

Juan went out back for a smoke and saw the flashing police lights down the street. He's the one who came in to spread the news and sounded the alarm.

"*La Migra* will kick in the back door any moment now," Carlos says. "Leaving is the only answer. If we go down the alley and over the fence, we can be on that other street before they get here."

Like most of the illegals, as soon as they were hired, they scouted the area for the best escape routes.

"If *La Migra* comes, you know they'll round us all up, throw us into detention, and deport us back to Mexico, Miguel. You *know* they will. They're doing it all over the country," Juan says, chewing on the fingernail on his right thumb.

My heart is pounding so hard I can hardly breathe. What to do? What to do? The one thing I know for sure is that if we do leave, we will never get our jobs back. I've been employed at Tony's for over four years, starting out as a dishwasher and working my way up to vegetable slicer and dicer, and now I prepare the salads.

The owner, Mr. Anthony, is a good boss. He pays us a decent wage and treats us fairly. But if we go, the chef will never hire us back. Even if Mr. Anthony insisted, Chef Alex would never agree. He hates Mexicans. Always yells at us, calls us names, says we're stupid and ignorant. He's even threatened us, saying that if we don't do exactly what he tells us to do, he's gonna call immigration and report us. He suspects one or two of us could be illegal. And even if Mr. Anthony forced him to take us back, the way the chef treats us now would be nothing like how he would treat us then. He'd make our lives a living hell. Everyone is afraid of him. Sometimes I'm tempted to tell Mr. Anthony, or maybe Louis, about the chef.

"Back to work, you idiots, and speak English!" he yells, and my friends scatter.

I agonize over what to do. I have papers, but will they stand up under the scrutiny of *la policia?* I bought them many years ago at the local flea market, just like most illegals. But now, things have changed. More and more of us are being deported. Years ago, it was only the criminals that immigration was after, but nowadays, ICE will kick in your door and deport you the next day, even if all you did was drive through a stop sign. It doesn't matter if you worked for the same company for the last ten years, paid your taxes, and had never been in any kind of real trouble. Before you know it, you're gone.

Yes, things are different now.

I look down at my work table, head bent low, afraid to read the fear in the eyes of my friends. I have a wife and two children. I can't afford to lose my job, but I can't afford to be deported back to Mexico, either.

I think about my life back there. My village was small, just a group of mud-brick huts. Dominating the center of town was the mandatory, ancient Catholic Church. The tiny general store also served as the local post office.

The only people living in the village were old men, women and children. All the able-bodied men had gone north to find work. It was that or sit and watch their children starve. So, every week, the women lined up at the post office. The lucky ones went home clutching envelopes of money, sent by husbands working up north, so their families could buy food.

The memories of my youth were fairly happy. I loved my mother and sister. And I was overjoyed when Papa came home to visit. However, in my fourteenth year, our envelopes from the north stopped, and my father never came home again. We never found out why. I knew then that I could never marry a girl from the village. It would mean living like Papa and the other men, going north for work and coming back every six or seven months to see my family. This wasn't what I wanted for myself or my family.

I walked into the ancient church and sought advice from my beloved priest, but Padre Martinez's advice was simply, "Pray, and God will provide the answers."

I knew my only chance for a better life lay north. So, along with prayer, I began gathering information from the village men whenever they came home, asking questions about their journeys and all the dangers.

Our village was about ten miles south of the Texas-Mexico border. Once across the Rio Grande, the nearest road was an additional ten miles or more over the hot, open desert.

I began to form a plan. When I was ready, I would join the men heading north.

At age seventeen, I kissed my mother and sister for what would be the last time and joined the small group of men headed for Laredo, Texas.

We left at twilight, trying to average three miles per hour. Once we reached the Rio Grande, we stopped, waiting for full-on darkness. Fortunately, there was no moon that night. Loaded down with jugs of water, we crossed the river at a spot that was low, thanks to the drought. Always on guard for signs of the border patrol, we moved quickly and quietly.

I drank sparingly in the desert, for running out of water could be a death sentence. As we drew further into the U.S., the men began to split up and it became every man for himself.

I was lucky. When I found the main road, I was picked up by an old Mexican man driving a beat up, gray pick-up who was also headed north.

Once on my own, I traveled as far away from the border as possible, working odd jobs—picking tomatoes, lettuce, peaches, whatever crop was in season—until I ended up here. I sent money back to my mother and my sister for years, but I could never go back.

My mother passed, and my sister married and moved to a bigger city. I still keep in touch with her, now by cellphone.

Then everything changed when the cartel took over the village.

The men could no longer return to visit their families without being forced to join the gangs. I tried to contact the few people I knew, but most have gone elsewhere. The last I heard, Padre Martinez had been murdered for preaching against the cartels.

I never stayed in one place too long, never wanted to attract too much attention. But living like that gets old, and I really liked this city and my job working construction. I decided to join a church, and that is where I first saw my Elena.

She was so beautiful. Her parents immigrated here legally, and she was born in the United States, and so is a citizen. Her family was not wealthy, but Elena was so smart. She got good grades in high school and even got a partial scholarship for college. She graduated with a degree in history and was an activist working for the Dreamers. We rarely spoke, though. I felt she would never be interested in me.

One Friday after work, I went to pick up my paycheck at the main construction site. I had worked there for two weeks. Construction work is hard—hauling bricks, lumber, unloading trucks. The foreman said they didn't owe me anything, because he didn't know who I was. He said I'd never worked there. I'd heard of this happening to other illegals, but it had never happened to me. What could I do? They knew I couldn't call the police and complain. They had seen my papers.

I told my friend what happened and somehow Elena heard about my problem. She wanted to know the name of the company. Through her work with the Dreamers, she was working with another organization that was going after companies like the one that had cheated me. She assured me my name would never be used.

After that, we became good friends and soon began dating. I never worked construction again. I learned to stick to working in hotels and restaurants.

Her parents weren't too happy when she decided to marry an uneducated kitchen worker, but Elena is strong willed. They finally accepted me and were overjoyed when we eventually presented them with two grandchildren. Both of my daughters are U.S. citizens. Elena works part-time as a teacher's assistant at the school that our girls attend, and is taking classes to get her teaching certificate.

Elena also has plans for me. Since she is an American, I have filed papers to become a citizen. That was three years ago, but the government keeps delaying the process. In the meantime, Elena had me enroll in English classes at our local church. My English is pretty good, but she thinks my vocabulary needs improvement.

And if she ever hears me say the words, "illegal aliens," she has a fit.

"Oh, you came here on a spaceship, did you?" she says.

According to American standards, our family doesn't have very much, but compared to my life in Mexico, we are rich. Elena and the girls could never come back with me to Mexico. I might not even survive back home with the cartels in charge.

My journey north took place years ago, before 9/11, and things have changed drastically since then. Once deported, there is no coming back. The border patrol has increased in numbers since then and they now have new fancy technology. Elena and the girls will have a hard time if I'm arrested. Money will be tight until she becomes a teacher. But she's strong and, most important, they belong here.

My friends Carlos and Juan approach my work table, interrupting my train of thought, and say, "Miguel, we're leaving. Are you coming with us?"

Carlos is my best friend. Our wives plan family barbeques together almost weekly. He's the chef's assistant, and is a great cook, always bringing something different but delicious to our house when we have a party. When I told him I'd love to be a cook too, and wished I was like him, he decided to teach me. Over the years, we've tried to see whose dishes were the best, even getting our guests to vote. At first Carlos always won, but little by little, I've been catching up.

"You can't leave, Carlos," I told him. "The chef will have a fit. He can't handle the Saturday night crowd all alone. He'll probably walk out too, but first he'll make sure you never get your job back. Even if Mr. Anthony wants to give you a second chance. This is a good job. You make good money here," I argue.

"What good is this job going to do me if *La Migra* catches us tonight and we all get deported? And you need to think about Elena and the girls. Don't be a fool, you need to come with us!" he pleads.

I only shake my head.

After they leave, the chef becomes very angry, yelling and cursing at all the workers.

"Where the hell is Carlos and that other guy?" he says. "I can't fill all of these orders by myself! Get me one of the waiters. Then get Anthony. He has to close down the restaurant until I get some help. Unless one of you idiots knows how to cook."

I have to help Mr. Anthony. I know he can't close down the restaurant. Without thinking, I say, "I do."

The chef walks towards me with a spatula in his hand and a menacing look on his face.

"What did you just say?" he says as he slaps the spatula against his palm in a steady beat.

"I said I know how to cook. Carlos and me are friends, and he taught me how to cook. He even taught me how to make those five sauces you make." I can feel my stomach clenching.

"You better not be lying to me. I'll have your head on a platter if you are. Get over here, stand in Carlos's spot. While I keep cooking, tell me about the sauces," he orders.

I take a deep breath and begin to recite what Carlos taught me.

"Sauce number one is butter and flour whisked with milk or cream—a cream sauce. Sauce number two is butter and flour whisked with a chicken broth. Sauce number three is a dark sauce. You need to brown the flour, not burn it. You whisk it with beef broth. Sauce number four is a tomato sauce. Sauce number five is from Holland and is egg yolks and butter," I rattle off, hoping I remembered it right.

The chef hands me a long, white apron and points to the large frying pan.

"I need a large cream sauce right now. And hurry," he shouts.

I drop two sticks of butter and rotate the pan, listening for the sizzle as the butter melts, just like Carlos showed me. Everyone in the kitchen freezes, holding their breath, their eyes glued to my hands.

Am I making the right decision? I'm not sure. Just an hour ago, I was making salads, and now everything depends on me making a cream sauce. Something that should be easy, but not under these conditions. I can see the chef has stopped what he was doing and is also staring at me....

I take another deep breath and decide to trust in the Virgin. I sprinkle the flour, grab the whisk, and blend it into the butter. I pick up the pitcher of milk and silently pray, "Hail Mary, full of grace..."

Laurel

WE SIT AT THE BAR, SIPPING OUR DRINKS, WAITING FOR A TABLE. IT'S Saturday night and I'm delighted to see how crowded it is. Business is finally back to normal since the reopening. In fact, we should have come earlier or made a reservation. It's cold and rainy outside, and it feels good to be where it's nice and warm.

We don't engage in small talk, haven't for years. So, I watch the handsome bartender hustle back and forth, serving his customers. He's good at his job—never forgets what you're drinking—and he's quite charming.

Our table is ready, so we sit down and retreat behind the safety of our menus. We started coming here when we were first married, almost thirty years ago. It was our favorite Italian restaurant. When young Anthony took over after his father passed away, I was afraid that he would make too many changes. The place closed for a few months, but after the renovations, it was more up-scale, elegant, and classier. Business seemed slower at first, yet the food remained first-rate; more eclectic, perhaps, but still excellent quality. We've never had a bad meal here.

So many years, where did they go?

He tries, "What are you going to have tonight?"

"The usual. You?"

"The same. Steak, rare. Baked potato."

"No vegetables or salad?" I smile and ask.

"A potato is a vegetable." He returns my smile.

He tries again. "So how was your week?"

"Fine, fine. Yours?"

"Good, good."

How long have we been like this? I look around the restaurant at all the couples joking and laughing; they don't seem to have any trouble communicating. When did we change?

Now I try, "How about the merger? Do you think it will go through?"

"It looks good. I don't foresee any problems."

"Oh, great."

When did talking become such hard work? It wasn't a problem when we were first married. We would interrupt, speak at the same time—we had so much to say. It wasn't a problem when the kids were at home. There was plenty of conversation then, too. Funny stories to share at dinner, their sporting events to discuss, vacations to plan. Words flew around the room and laughter reverberated throughout the house. Where did it all go?

Perhaps it was when we lost Tyler. In our pain, did we turn away, instead of toward each other? The death of a child has broken up so many marriages. I always thought we were different. Maybe I was wrong.

I try again. "The Jacksons called. They want to know if we'll come over for dinner next Saturday."

He looks up. "Sure, great, sounds good."

"They probably want to talk about their latest cruise," I chuckle.

"That's right, they travel all the time, don't they?" He checks his cell phone.

When did *we* stop traveling? We used to go everywhere—Europe, Hawaii, the Caribbean, so many cruises. Now we spend every vacation visiting the children. Do we need to be surrounded by family in order to enjoy ourselves? Does the thought of spending time together alone on a trip frighten us? At home, we usually retreat to the safety of our separate offices.

He tries once more. "We really should paint the house this spring."

"So soon?" I say, genuinely surprised.

"Well, it's been five years."

"Five years. Where did the time go?"

I watch the flickering candle in the center of the table. In our silence, we avoid eye contact. Would it be too easy to see the loss? I stop and gaze at him across the table, really trying to see him.

I'm surprised to see how much grayer he's gotten, how many more creases line his face. I have chronicled every one of my gray hairs and wrinkles, but not his. How sad that I never noticed. He's such a good man. And to be honest, at fifty-five, he's still quite attractive.

We were happy once. Were we just so busy that we let it all slip through our fingers?

The first indication I had that our marriage might be in trouble was about three years ago. I was having lunch with my old college friend, Nicole Roberts. She and I try to meet in town at least three times a year. We shop for shoes and the latest fashions, and always end up sharing a late lunch at one of the top five-star restaurants.

I've always greatly admired Nicole. She's one of those women who has been able to stay happily married, raise two children, and manage a full-time job. She has on occasion admitted that she paid a price for her success, like sacrificing time spent with her children. She once even admitted that she envied the years I spent at home with my family.

I've never regretted being a stay-at-home mom while the children were young, waiting to pick up my career until they were out of high school. And I've done really well in the business world despite my late start.

As one of our luncheons drew to an end, Nicole seemed uncomfortable.

"I don't know if I should mention this or not," she started. "But if it was my husband, I'd really want to know."

"Know about what?" I asked.

"Last month, when I was in Chicago, I was staying at the Ritz. I was just finishing breakfast with a few business associates when I saw Jonathan enter the restaurant with another woman. It was obvious they were staying at the hotel together because, from where I was sitting, I saw them exit the elevator together. She was in her late twenties, tall, thin, shoulder length blond hair, extremely attractive. I was on the other side of the room, and he didn't notice me. I hesitated to approach him. When our bill came, I just left with my colleagues."

I started to chuckle. "Oh, Nicole, that's just Tiffany, his administrative assistant. She often travels with him, especially when they're negotiating a big contract or a merger. She's the nicest girl, I've met her several times."

"Are you kidding me? If she was Jerod's assistant, I'd be doing everything in my power to get rid of her. Don't you ever worry about something going on between the two of them? Jonathan is only human, and she is really very attractive," Nicole stated.

"Were they holding hands?" I laughed.

"No, but she seemed to be hanging on his every word."

"Jonathan says Tiffany is a very smart woman. She's ambitious and anxious to learn everything he can teach her about how the company operates. He's really impressed with her."

"I don't know which is more dangerous—a smart blonde or a dumb blonde. But I do know an ambitious blonde can definitely be trouble," Nicole said. "You can't help but wonder, does she want to get ahead in the company, or does she want to be a part owner?"

"Nicole, stop it. I'm not worried. I trust Jonathan."

"I know you do. But do you trust Tiffany?" Nicole raised her eyebrows.

I just laughed, but Nicole's parting words should have caused me some concern.

"Be careful, Laurel, you don't want to end up in divorce court at our age."

Later that night, I thought about Tiffany. She was just as attractive as Nicole pointed out and really quite charming. But I realized that the thought of Jonathan having an affair didn't upset me nearly as much as it should have. A few years earlier, I would have been frantic at the thought of losing him. Instead, I just brushed aside Nicole's warning as being silly.

"Jeff called today," Jonathan says with a smile, bringing me back to the present.

"Really? What's up?" I smile in reply.

"Just some questions about the business. But he also said that he and Jan will be coming home for Thanksgiving, if that's okay." Now the smile reaches his eyes.

"Of course, that's okay! I'll give him a call first thing in the morning. See what their plans are."

"I told him it was fine, but you better call him and back me up. Why don't you call Nancy—see if they can come too?" he suggests.

"That's a great idea. I'll call her right after I talk to Jeff. Then I'll call you and let you know what she says." I smile and feel a spark of excitement.

We love when the children come home. The house is filled with conversation and laughter—all the things that are missing when we're alone. It's remarkable how much he finds to talk about and do with them. He discusses sports with Jeff, plays with the grandchildren—he seems really happy.

What are we going to do about the elephant that's in the room right now? We have walked around it for years, but lately it seems so much larger. Do I simply say, *Jonathan, I want a divorce. I don't love you anymore?*

How would he react? Will he be angry, blame me and give me a lecture? Will he be relieved or indifferent? Will he tell me about another woman he's met? Wouldn't that be wonderful? I may not love him anymore, but I still think that Jonathan deserves to be happy. He deserves a woman who will love him the way I used to.

Will I say, *We'll be much better off apart?* Is that even true? Sadly, I'm afraid it is.

The one thing I know about Jonathan is that down deep, he is a realist. Sooner or later, he'll grab one of his large yellow legal pads and his gold pen and start a list.

What will we do about the house? I certainly don't want to stay there all by myself. It's too big and there are too many memories. I doubt he will, either. He's never been that wrapped up in it. Whenever I wanted to make any improvements, his solution was always to just hire someone to do it. In all the years we've been married, I never saw Jonathan with a hammer or a paint brush in his hand.

We certainly have enough furniture and possessions to outfit two apartments or townhouses. Maybe we'll start by going through our antiques. Perhaps we'll both want that blue and white vase we bought in Chinatown on one of our trips to San Francisco. Money won't be a problem. We both have great jobs and our own money.

I hope it doesn't turn ugly. But if I haven't cared enough to argue for ages, why start now?

Thanksgiving is only a couple of weeks away. I guess I'll have to put the elephant back in the closet for a while. I wonder if the children can see him too.

Whenever they visit, they always ask me how I am with a hint of concern in their eyes. Do they see how distant their dad and I have become? How do we tell them? Do we sit at the Thanksgiving table, drinking coffee and eating our pumpkin pie, and say, "Oh, by the way, Dad and I are getting a divorce?" I think not.

I remember last year when I found the lump in my breast. I scheduled the biopsy, awaited the results and was overjoyed when they came back benign. Sitting in my office, I realized there was no one to celebrate with. I had gone through the whole ordeal alone. It never crossed my mind to turn to Jonathan for support or comfort. My only thought was that I didn't want to bother him. I couldn't believe I had grown that emotionally distant from my own husband. That was the day I began to re-evaluate my life.

The Monday after Thanksgiving, we are going to confront the elephant. I want to sit across from Jonathan and express my feelings as calmly and honestly as possible. I hope the pain I inflict won't be too shocking. I can't believe how much lighter I feel already, how free—almost happy.

I look across the table and know it's time. We both need to get on with our lives.

But for now, all I say is, "Should we have dessert?"

Brad

"What do you mean, you can't tell her?!" I drop my silverware just as I was about to cut into my last bite of prime rib and watch Oliver's ever-present tan slowly begin to fade.

"Lower your voice," he whispers, his eyes darting from side to side. "Please don't cause a scene."

I follow suit and find the only other table paying us any attention is the one with the two older guys and the blonde chick in the red satin outfit with the extremely short skirt. They look as much out of place here tonight as I feel. Tony's is our favorite restaurant, and we come here often. And Oliver would be mortified if I raised my voice.

He hates it when I display any emotion. Oliver is always in control of his feelings, not like me. They say opposites attract. And I am certainly Oliver's opposite. I have no trouble showing when I'm angry, but I try never to embarrass him. He doesn't want people staring at us.

As if they ever stare at *us.* When I'm with him, I could just as soon be invisible. Oliver is *gorgeous*—movie star gorgeous. If he wasn't brilliant and hadn't devoted his life to the law, I'm sure he would have ended up in Hollywood. I can never understand how he manages to look so immaculate. Like now: a two-hour delay at the airport, a three-hour flight and still his suit looks like he just picked it up at the dry cleaner—the crease in his trousers knife-sharp, no wrinkles anywhere, the knot of his tie exactly where it's supposed to be, his hair perfect, not a lock out of place. As perfect as he looks in jeans and a t-shirt.

Don't get me wrong. It's not like I'm a dog, or anything. At different stages of my life, I've even been considered downright handsome. I'm almost tall—five feet, eleven inches—blond, blue-eyed, physically fit. I played soccer in college. It's just that everyone is mesmerized by Oliver, just like I was from the first moment I met him at that Christmas party.

I spotted him right away across the room—tall, six feet, four inches, jet-black hair, dark, dark brown eyes, square jawed, with a cleft in his chin. I was drawn to him right away. I remember thinking he looked a lot like Superman. But right now, I'm too angry to be mesmerized.

"Just let me explain," Oliver pleads. He's nervous. I can tell because he's worrying one of his gold cufflinks, a habit he had successfully broken—until now.

I push back into my seat and offer him no help. I'm about to fold my arms across my chest when I stop. Oliver and I understand enough about body language to know that would signal a closed mind, so I fold them in my lap. Of course, down deep, I know my mind is closed. But I'm determined to act calm and modulate my voice.

"Please, go right ahead," I say, smiling. "Why don't you start at the beginning, in case I missed something the first time?"

I catch the eye of our favorite waitress and indicate I'd like another drink. Oliver shakes his head.

"Don't drink too much tonight, Brad." Oliver frowns.

"Since when has two drinks ever put me under the table?" I say as sarcastically as possible.

"Brad, don't be like that." He pauses, then: "The law firm was great. The partners were very gracious. I nailed the interview." He does a quick fist pump. "Different partners took me out each night, so I got acquainted with most of the team where I'd be assigned. You're going to love San Francisco—the restaurants, the night life. And several members of the firm are our kind of people…"

"You mean they're gay?" I ask, surprised.

"Brad, stop it," Oliver orders.

"Oh, I'm sorry," I say almost—but not really—apologetically. "I mean *diversified.*"

Oliver just ignores me. "And I showed you the offer they made me. We'll never have to worry about money again. I would be practicing only criminal law, no more civil cases. It's what I've always wanted—you know that." He rearranges the silverware on his side of the table, an effort to release some of his pent-up, nervous energy.

"I know," I say, nodding and smiling. "It sounds like your dream job. I'm happy for you Oliver, I really am. So what about real estate? Did you get to look at any houses while you were there?"

"Not really. Housing is a problem. The market is sky high. I did visit some luxury high rise condos. Several of them were amazing. Floor to ceiling windows, views of the Bay, Golden Gate Bridge. I even toured some of them at night and the views were breathtaking."

He is so animated and excited that I hate to ask the next question because I already know the answer.

"And were they two or three bedrooms?"

Oliver realizes too late that he's walked right into my trap. Foolish for a top-rated lawyer.

He hesitates, then says, "Mostly two. I think I saw one with three bedrooms. But it didn't have a view."

"Oh, and you wouldn't want an apartment without a view, would you? So, the two bedrooms, they would be what, the master and a guest room? Because we have to have a guest room, right?" I ask, in all innocence.

"Yes, of course, it's San Francisco, I'm sure a lot of people will want to come visit us." He laughs.

"Yeah, my brothers, your sister, my mom, your mom. And therein lies the problem. Doesn't it? What do we do with good old Brad when your mom comes to town? Do we stick him in a hotel somewhere?"

Before I can go on, I'm interrupted.

"Would either of you gentlemen like a refill?" asks our favorite waitress.

I down the rest of my drink, smile and say, "Thanks Kelly, I'll take another scotch on the rocks. I'd also like a piece of your famous key lime pie and a cup of black coffee."

Oliver is glaring at me and I can see the anger bubbling up inside him, tightening the muscles in his jaw, at my ordering a third drink. He wants to finish this discussion in private, and he's wrestling to control his feelings. But I've learned a lot living with a lawyer for over five years. I prefer neutral ground.

"I'm fine Kelly, nothing for me," Oliver calmly says as he flashes his famous smile.

"Well, Brad." The smooth lawyer begins to plead his case. "I thought you could get a small apartment nearby."

"And how am I supposed to pay for that? I don't have a job waiting for me, do I?" It's getting harder for me to stay calm.

"I'll have plenty of money, I'll pay for it." He smiles and throws his hands out, palms up.

"Oh, that's right. How stupid of me. We'll also need a place to store all my computer equipment when your mom comes. In fact, those guest rooms probably aren't very big. We don't want to be carting all that equipment back and forth every time we have a party. So, we rent Brad a small apartment, set up his computers, and then he can work there, just like he does now. And then he'd only be at the high rise when it's convenient for you." I am grinding my teeth and let my sarcasm echo.

"It's not like that at all and you know it," Oliver says. "And besides, you'll get a job in no time. I'm sure the firm has contacts in the technology industry. You could even get a real job working in an office so you wouldn't need all that computer equipment of yours. You could sell most of it and just carry a laptop, like most people." Oliver is smiling more naturally now.

"Do you even know me, Oliver? I love what I do. Do you even know that I own the company I work for? I enjoy going into new start-up companies, meeting with the personnel and designing custom-made computer systems to meet their individual needs. I love making house calls to senior citizens who have messed up their Microsoft program and don't know what to do. I'm a magician, as far as they're concerned. I would hate being stuck in an office. And as for all that computer equipment you so nonchalantly said 'I could just sell,' it took me *years* to finance the purchase of those machines." I notice my voice is getting louder.

"Okay, okay. You can work wherever you want. Maybe we can even rent you a nice office somewhere in one of those historic buildings. The choice is yours. You just don't understand about my mother. It will break her heart when I tell her," Oliver insists.

"Oh, I understand completely. We all take a risk when we tell the truth. I thought my dad actually loved me, but he has not spoken to me since the day I came out. He says he'll go to his grave that way. I was sure I had also broken my mother's heart that day, but once she was over the shock, she called and said she loved me before I came out and she'd always love me. I underestimated her. She loves me enough to stand up to my father and accept me for who I am. So, don't tell me I don't understand, Oliver. And your mother loves you too. You just don't have the courage to trust that love."

"But my family is much more conservative than yours and more religious," Oliver says. "My grandfather was a bishop, and my dad and his brothers were all deacons. They would all disown me."

"All these years and I didn't know I was living with a member of the church hierarchy. And how come I've never met any of these ultraconservative members of your family at your family functions?" I ask.

"They are on my father's side of the family."

"Correct me if I'm wrong, but aren't they the ones your mother can't stand?"

Oliver has the decency to look embarrassed and nods his head.

"So, this sounds to me like just another lame excuse not to come out to your mother."

"No, it's not that. Life in San Francisco is going to be great, Brad. You'll love it there. I know you will. Let's fly up next weekend and look around. It's one of the most scenic cities in the United States. We'll ride the trolley cars, eat on Fisherman's Wharf. We can go to Chinatown, Alcatraz…"

"Oliver, Oliver, stop! I was moving to San Francisco to get married, buy a house, raise a family, live a normal life, just like Roger and William and our other friends, like their next-door neighbors. You know that's what I've looked forward to. Don't you see? You're asking me to sell my company, desert all my seniors, leave my friends and my whole family. For what? The same life I have here, except in a much smaller apartment. I love you, Oliver, but I want more, the kind of more you're not interested in. And I think you care more about your mother than you do me."

I sigh and continue, "I wish you luck in Frisco, I really do. I hope you achieve everything you've ever dreamed of. But me, I'm out—more than just out of the closet."

"Brad, don't do this! I do love you." Oliver looks awful—so sad.

"Yes, you love me as much as you know how," I say. "But it's not enough. It's my turn to pick up the check tonight but I'm gonna let you get it. After all, you're rich now."

I reclaim my raincoat—the one Oliver gave me for my birthday last year—and head for the foyer. I've always been a big fan of the rain, but not so much on the worst night of my life.

It might just be my imagination, but as I turn up my collar, I swear that handsome new blond waiter winks at me. We share a smile. I flip my collar up around my neck and head out the front door, laughing.

Maybe there is life after Oliver.

Darlene

THE MAÎTRE D' SHOWS US TO OUR USUAL TABLE, AND I AM SO ANGRY. Dinner and drinks at my favorite restaurant, and you've ruined it already. I'm so mad, and you don't even know it. You just sit there, blissfully reading the menu with no idea how badly you've hurt my feelings. You haven't even noticed that I stopped talking to you about twenty-five minutes ago. Lucky for you, I absolutely refuse to make a scene in a public place. But I swear, I just want to scream.

Why can't you read me? I can read you. When you walk in the back door, I check your face, the slope of your shoulders. Do you look tired, tense, stressed? Is there a spring in your step? I can tell if you've had a good day or a bad day. Why can't you do the same?

When we were first married, I got really upset with you once and you said, "I'm not a mind reader." I thought you had a point, so I've tried to articulate since then. I tell you what I want or don't want, what I need and don't need. But I've looked in the mirror when I'm angry. I've seen how pinched and tense I look. I know you're not a mind reader, but did you forget to tell me that you're also blind?

Oh, what's the use? You'll never change. But why not? I have. I've learned to care less and less about me and more and more about you. I've learned to flex, to bend. Why haven't you?

Oh Jesus, you're making a toast.

"To us," you say.

I smile. How sweet? Us, what us? Can't you see I'm about to walk out?

And I can just hear your mother when you tell her I've left you. "I told you not to marry her. I never liked her. She doesn't keep the house as clean as I would have."

I always felt like she was checking for dust whenever she and your step-dad were over. And I usually got the impression that she never approved of what I served for dinner. Like when I served chicken, I really should have served beef. When I first met her, I didn't realize she could be so opinionated. I have to admit, I will really miss your step-dad, though. Such a sweetheart. He always makes me laugh.

And tonight, when we have this argument—and, believe me, we will have this argument—I know exactly what you will say.

"I work hard every week to support you and the kids. Do you think I enjoy all the traveling I have to do, sleeping in hotels, eating every meal all by myself in restaurants? And you know I don't screw around. What more do you want?"

Well, to be honest, I think you do enjoy all that traveling. I know I wouldn't mind spending some time all alone in a hotel room, once in a while. And what do I want? I'll tell you what I want. I want you to see me, hear me, pay attention to me. Take tonight. I know exactly what you'll order. And you'll have no idea what I want.

You'll say, "What are you gonna have tonight, honey?" Even though I order the same thing every time we come here. Just once, I wish you would remember that I love lasagna.

But more importantly, tonight we have to discuss how you have changed. You've been a great dad so far. You never hesitated to change a diaper. On the weekends, you even took the midnight feedings so I could get some sleep. You always helped in any way you could. But now that the boys are older, you seem to have adopted the "good cop, bad cop" method of discipline. And I have become the perennial bad cop. I know you were raised by a single mom. And maybe never having had a dad around when you were young, you think you should be the boys' best friend.

Believe me, Teddy and Greg are very charming, and they're going to have plenty of best friends in their lives. But they'll only have one dad, David, and that's you. They need you to fill that role. Every time I tell them they can't do something, they run to you. If you overrule me, you undermine my authority. The boys are losing respect for me and when you aren't home, I'm having trouble getting them to behave. Statements like *we guys have to stick together* are hurtful, even though I know that's not your intention. I just hope I can make you understand that I want you and I to work as a team, not with you guys ganged up against me. We both know parenting isn't easy, and I want us to work this out together.

And do you think you're the only one who works hard? Who do you think does all the laundry, cleans the house and cooks all the meals? I do all the grocery shopping; I buy all of the boy's clothes—and most of yours, I might add. I drive the boys everywhere they have to go: school functions, ball practice, doctors and dentist appointments. I don't remember ever calling you out of a meeting to chauffeur the kids.

Not to mention, I'd pay money to watch you endure one single labor pain or see you give birth just once. Every time you get sick, you're such a baby. You lie around expecting me to wait on you hand and foot.

And remember, I had a perfectly good job before I met you. I was a paralegal. I made plenty of money. I could buy all the clothes I wanted without anyone asking me how much they cost. I loved living in my nice, little apartment and driving my mini-car. On our first date I even told you I had no intentions of getting married. I loved my job and enjoyed being single.

Now you have gone to the men's room and you're taking your time. I have to close my eyes and take deep breaths. I'm giving myself a headache.

Correction, *you're* giving me a headache.

It's really raining tonight. I look around the restaurant. We've been coming here for years. It's the type of place you come to relax, unwind, and enjoy the great food. Well, I guess not tonight. It's Saturday night, so all the tables are taken. I'm glad I don't see anyone we know. I'm not in the mood to socialize.

To think, I put on a nice dress; got my hair and nails done just for this. I think I'll order another drink, try to calm down.

I wish I had a pair of scissors so I could cut you out like a huge paper doll. I'd roll you up and throw you in the trash. No, better still, I wish I had a giant, pink eraser and starting at the top, I could slowly and carefully erase every bit of you. Then I could sit here and enjoy my drink across the table from a big, vacant space that would probably be better company.

I must be losing my mind, sitting here all by myself, trying not to burst out laughing. I've painted a visual picture that I can't get out of my mind. What is the matter with me? I've just sat here and erased the only man I've ever loved.

When we first began to date, I was so adamant that I would never marry. I even told you the stories the ladies at work shared about the horrors of being soccer moms. But when I fell in love with you, I thought you'd never propose. The day you told me to dress extra fancy because we were meeting an old college friend of yours at the Hilton restaurant, I thought nothing of it. And when you said he texted to say he wasn't going to make it, I felt so sorry that you had missed out on seeing your old friend. But when you jumped out of your seat, got down on one knee and flashed a satin box, offering me the ring that now sits on my left hand, I was stunned—utterly speechless. I could tell by the look on your face, you thought I was going to turn you down. But I was so excited that I threw myself into your arms and almost knocked us both onto the floor. I had never been so happy.

You're the man I've been married to for twelve years, the father of my children, a man who loves me. Granted, you're thoughtless and oblivious. But you're mine, damn it, and I love you. And after we have our talk, maybe I'll even share my plan with the pink eraser with you. You'll get a kick out of that one.

But now you sit back down, and completely cover up the vacant hole. And I look at you, really look at you. You flash that great smile, the one that is so contagious. You reach across the table and squeeze my hand.

"Hey, my mom called me today," you say. "She and Carl have come up with this great idea. They are going to rent a house for two months this summer on Amelia Island, off the northernmost tip of Florida. We'd have to fly into Jacksonville, drive up the coast and take a ferry to get there. They want you, me and the boys to come and stay for two weeks. She's planned a side trip to Orlando so we can all go to Disney World. Wouldn't the boys love that?"

"Yeah," I say, kind of shocked.

"They know I can't stay longer than two weeks because I don't get any extra time off this summer, but they want you and the boys to stay as long as you'd like. Mom said she and Carl know how hard you work, with the boys being so active and all. They thought this would be a great opportunity for you to get some rest. They'd take the boys sight-seeing, to the beach, stuff like that. The house has a pool so you could swim or just lay out there, relax and read a book. You know they are both crazy about you. My mom always says I couldn't have picked a better wife. And of course, they adore the boys. What do you say?"

"Your mom said all that? I always thought she liked your ex-girlfriend Vickie much better than she likes me," I say, totally confused.

"You've got to be kidding me! Vickie was always talking about New York City. She wanted to move there ever since she was in high school. My mom was petrified that if I married her, she'd talk me into moving across the country too. Then she'd never see me or her grandchildren, if she and I ever had any kids. When I started dating you, she liked that you were such an independent woman. You know how big my mom was in the women's movement back in the sixties. Plus, you have that big family right here in town and you all are so close. She figured you wouldn't be pushing me to move anywhere. And the more she got to know you, she thought you were perfect for me. She was so happy when I told her I was going to propose. Even though I wasn't so sure you were going to say yes. So, what do you think? It's up to you. Should I tell my mom we're thrilled, or would you rather we pass?"

"Are you serious? It sounds wonderful! I just can't believe that all this time I thought your mother didn't like me." I feel awful. I slouch down in my chair, put my elbow on the table and place my head in my left hand. I have got to be nicer to David's mother.

"Oh, don't worry about it," David says. "She thinks you don't like her, either. But I told her it was just her imagination. So, are you gonna order your usual tonight, honey? Lasagna, right?" He smiles.

"Yep, that's right." I smile back.

Richard

I CHECK MY WATCH AND LOOK TOWARD THE DOOR AGAIN. SHE'S LATE, AS usual. As always. You'd think I'd be used to it by now, but I'm not. It's so annoying. After all, she is a grown woman. All she has to do is check the diamond Rolex I gave her for her birthday. But no. She'll come breezing in, making no excuses, loaded down with packages. She's out shopping; spending my money. She never has any trouble doing that. I check my cell—no text or email.

She usually isn't this late, and considering the weather, I begin to worry. The roads can be treacherous on a rainy night like this. I wonder at what point I should call the police. No, I'm just being silly. She will show up soon. In she'll come, beautiful, elegant, her lovely auburn hair floating around her shoulders, and she'll turn every head in the place. That is the one part of the evening I'll particularly enjoy. When the customers realize which table she's headed toward, every man in the restaurant will think, *lucky bastard,* and every woman, *dirty old man.* But I don't care.

Finally, she sails in, as predicted, her gorgeous hair glistening with rain. She looks like she just stepped out of *Vogue* magazine, wearing a gray suit with a long, gray plaid cape. I don't know much about fashion but I thought gray was supposed to be a dull color. But on her, it's magical. As expected, she carries several packages—there's always time to shop.

She reaches the table, bends down and kisses me on the check.

"Hi Daddy. Sorry I'm late."

"You're always late." I try to sound gruff, but she can hear the smile in my voice. It's hard to believe this beautiful woman is my little girl.

"I had some shopping to do. You wouldn't want a girl to look shabby now, would you?" she laughs.

"You haven't looked shabby since you were fifteen years old," I reply.

I remember when she was ten years old and didn't care what she looked like, hair in braids and clothes that didn't match. Where did my little tomboy go?

She's just two years out of college and working her first job. I'll continue her allowance until she gets on her feet—only the best for my baby girl. She babbles on about her job, her many friends. Throwing around names that I guess I'm supposed to recognize but don't. If I ask, she will just frown and tell me I never listen.

We have met for dinner twice a month ever since the divorce. We rotate restaurants, but I know Tony's is one of her favorites.

"I'm starving, haven't eaten since lunch," she murmurs as she scans the menu. The food here is outstanding, and for a thin woman, she really loves to eat.

"How is your mother?" I ask. "Is she dating at all?"

She gives me that disapproving look and says, "Mom is fine, and you know I don't discuss her personal life, that's one of the rules."

Ah, the rules. She laid them out as a teenager during our first dinner and has kept to them religiously. She doesn't know that I still love her mother, never asked who caused the divorce—another one of her rules. She refuses to take sides, luckily for me.

"So, how is Tom?" I ask in all innocence.

"Daddy, I haven't seen Tom in almost a year," she frowns. "You never pay attention."

Beth orders her favorite chicken marsala and I stick with my standard steak. You can't go wrong with Tony's steaks. I order a small bottle of wine and try to make amends.

"Is your salad okay?" I ask as I pour our wine.

"It's fine," she smiles.

I realize that Thanksgiving is just over two weeks away and steer the subject in that direction. When Carolyn and I divorced, we agreed to keep Beth's life as normal as possible. So, in spite of the past, every holiday the three of us celebrate just like a regular family. And we have managed to pull it off quite well. I really look forward to Thanksgiving. Beth and her mother will cook tons of food, more than an army could consume: turkey, all the trappings, and their wonderful pumpkin pie. I'll get to enjoy a great home-cooked meal for a change.

"Thanksgiving is coming up," I comment. "I assume it's at your mother's house."

"Yes," she replies. "I need to talk to you about that."

I don't like the sound of that, but wait for her to finish.

"There will be an extra person at dinner. I'm bringing my friend Martin. You'll really like him, he's a neurosurgeon. I met him at Melinda's birthday party. I want you to be nice to him. I'm serious Daddy, he's really wonderful." There's a sparkle in her eyes.

"When haven't I been nice to your friends?" I ask.

"Well, there was that guy in high school you wouldn't let in the front door and you kept hanging up on," she laughs.

"That was a long time ago. If you really like him, I'm sure I will, too," I say, trying to be honest.

This is the moment every father dreads. Bad enough they grow up so fast, but sooner or later they find someone "really wonderful."

I cut another piece of my steak and say, "So, tell me more about Martin."

"He's amazing. Right after Thanksgiving he's leaving on a medical mission to Kenya. Martin always knew he wanted to be a surgeon, even when he was a kid. He used to bombard his G.P. with questions whenever his mom brought him in for a visit. His doctor even became his mentor. He brought him to the hospital once to observe the surgery of an infant with a cleft palate. He became so inspired by that surgery that he included pediatric ear, nose and throat surgery in his residency and did a one-year fellowship in that specialty. He goes on a mission every year to operate on children in Africa who have no access to that type of surgery."

I watch the light in her eyes and sip my wine. This isn't looking good. I had so hoped this might be a passing infatuation. But it turns out, Martin is a saint.

"So, I guess he's a lot older than you are," I say casually.

"No, Daddy. Martin graduated high school when he was sixteen. He had taken all advanced classes and in college he majored in premed and graduated in three years. Can you imagine that? It took me over five years to graduate," she says, smiling.

"Yes, I remember. It wasn't an academic problem. There was that semester that you simply *had* to study in Paris, and all those classes that you took because they sounded *sooo* interesting and had nothing to do with your major. For a while there, I thought you were going to be a professional student." I laugh too.

Beth throws back her head and laughs out loud, that laugh that sounds more like music, attracting several stares.

"Well, anyway, he aced his MCAT and was the youngest student in his class at medical school. After that, he did a six-year residence and a two-year fellowship, so he's only seven years older than I am. He can't wait to meet you. You will have so much to talk about!"

Great! She's not only in love with a saint, he's also a genius. I'm sure a neurosurgeon who is changing lives in Africa is going to have a lot to say to a residential architectural engineer.

"Are you listening? Martin is a World War II buff just like you are. The first time I walked into his office, it was just like walking into yours. One whole wall is bookcases filled with the same books as you have, about every World War II battle, all the generals. I felt like I was back in school, borrowing one of them to work on a term paper for American history. He's anxious to see all of your war memorabilia that I told him about. I know you are both going to get along famously."

"I'm sure we are, honey," I agree.

"Hey, Dad, how did you know when you were in love, I mean really in love, like with Mom?" I'm surprised that Beth looks so vulnerable.

"Well, I always thought I knew exactly what I wanted in a partner. I only dated tall, blonde girls, and I liked the kind that were sweet and compliant. You know, the kind of girls who were easy to get along with. Don't give me that look. I'm not talking about sex. I'm talking about girls that wouldn't argue with me all the time."

"You mean girls that would put up with your crap," Beth laughs.

"That's not what I said, Beth. But maybe you're right. I was a college kid at the time. So, anyway, one night I was at this frat party and across the room I saw this young, petite redhead standing with a group of students. They were all laughing; she said something and everyone burst out laughing. Every time I looked her way, she seemed to be laughing and having so much fun. I just had to meet her. I remember thinking, I'd love to spend time with someone who seemed to enjoy life as much as she did.

"I don't think I really believe in love at first sight, but I certainly do believe in attraction at first sight. Well, I made my way over and got someone I knew to introduce me. We began talking and I tried some of my best lines on her. She just blew me off, practically told me to get lost. I knew I was going to have to work harder to get her to go out with me. I even went so far as to find out what classes she was signing up for that next semester and made sure I'd just happen to be in some of the same classes. It took me a whole year, but she finally came around and agreed to go out with me. She was something else, and she certainly lived up to that red hair. She absolutely didn't take my crap, Beth. I proposed right after graduation. I was crazy about your mom," I laugh.

"Oh, you two! Mom told me she had seen you around campus and knew she had to play hard-to-get to attract you. She said you had dated so many girls in all the sororities so she knew she had to be different. She said she held out as long as she could. She was crazy about you, too. You know Dad, I've never asked about your breakup, but after hearing the way you guys talk about each other, it seems like you both found true love. One of you or both of you screwed it up. You should talk to each other after Thanksgiving. Maybe it's not too late to find it again."

She's too young to realize that not all love stories have happy endings. That not all mistakes can be forgiven. And I'm not willing to be the one to explain those facts of life to her. Carolyn and I will meet Martin. We'll be sincerely warm and friendly, just the way Beth wants, just as we've been since our divorce. But there will be no talk of reconciliation. No matter how much I love her mother, that boat sailed years ago.

She's getting ready to leave now. She hesitates as if she wants to say something else but decides against it. There are places to go, things to do, and she's probably late.

She kisses me on the cheek saying, "See you Thanksgiving. Two o'clock. Don't be late," and flies out the door, leaving admiring glances in her wake.

I guess before I know it, she and her mother will be planning a huge wedding that will cost me a fortune. Can I bear to walk her down the aisle and give my precious girl away? I'm not sure. I wish she was still little. Life was so much simpler then. I wish I hadn't made so many mistakes.

I signal for the check and visualize all that beautiful auburn hair surrounded by a white veil.

Millie

I SIT AND WATCH ANGELO, OUR BUSBOY, CLEAR AWAY OUR DINNER DISHES and Sam, our waiter, hand out the dessert menus, which isn't necessary since we all have them memorized. The portions at Tony's are generous enough to allow each of us to take home enough lasagna or veal parmesan for another meal. Even though I'm stuffed and always trying to lose weight, I never turn down my monthly splurge with my friends. Each trip, I vow to order a large slice of their decadent chocolate cake, but never can resist another serving of Mama's famous rice pudding piled high with whipped cream.

Our group has reserved this table over in the corner once a month for the past eighteen years. In the beginning, we met on Tuesday, when our membership was much larger, because it was their slowest night of the week. But they changed to Saturday nights as our group became more popular and we wanted the meetings to be more special. It also gave us an excuse to get dressed up.

Mama and I were two of the founding members of the Women of a Certain Age Book Club. Members had to be sixty or older to join. All of us were from the neighborhood and most of us had been friends for years.

Tony insisted that Mama take time away from work to attend our meetings, even though she often would hurry into the back to oversee some crisis. We joked we should have set our tables up in the kitchen. Poor Carmen never really had time to finish the books. Between the restaurant and her children and grandchildren, she'd squeeze in the first few chapters and then a couple of days before our meetings, the end. But oh, how we'd laugh at all her questions about what happened in between. She was my dear friend and I still miss her so much.

We took a break while the restaurant was closed, and I wasn't sure if the new Tony's would accommodate us any longer, even though our numbers had dwindled down to four. Just before the grand re-opening, I passed by and noticed young Anthony working inside. I gathered all my courage and knocked on the door. He seemed so happy to see me and he brought me inside to show me around the place, and I really was impressed. The changes were amazing.

I knew Carmen would have been so proud of what he accomplished, and I told him so. He even had tears in his eyes. Anthony had always been such a good boy. Finally, I decided to be brave.

"Anthony," I said. "I don't know if the book club is something you would rather not have meeting in the new restaurant. We would be willing to meet on another day. One that isn't as busy as a Saturday night." I know I was biting my lip because that's what I do when I'm nervous.

He just stepped forward and grabbed me in a huge hug.

"Mrs. Gardner, that table in the corner is reserved for the book club, the second Saturday night of every month for as long as you want it." He pointed to the same alcove that was there before the renovations.

"I know how much my mom loved book club," he continued. "I was hoping you might be adding more members one of these days. Our new neighbors, their mother lives with them now and she's in her seventies. I was gonna ask you ladies if she could join—that's if she's interested, of course."

He smiled. I couldn't wait to get home and call all the ladies.

Once our desserts, coffee and second glasses of wine are served, I call our meeting to order and explain the rules, the ones that everyone knows.

"As per tradition, we'll go around the table and everyone will give us their impression of the book. Agreed?" Everyone dutifully nods their heads.

"Frances?" I look at the tall, distinguished looking woman with salt and pepper hair that's pulled back in a French twist. She has dark, almost black, eyes, wears minimal make-up, and is sitting to my left. She's dressed in a gray tweed suit with a white shell.

"I really enjoyed the book," she says, smiling. "The ending caught me by surprise. But I thought the author's use of language was amazing and his descriptions of the scenery were beautiful. The way he captured the character's emotions was so realistic."

Frances is by far the most educated of us, but has a wonderful sense of humor.

"You always diagnose the language. that's because you were a teacher," Marlene says, frowning. And we all chuckle.

"Well, what did you think, Marlene?" I ask the short, shapely woman sitting across from me. She, like me, keeps her short, colored blond hair in the latest style. She has always been the most attractive one in our group. She has taken classes on applying make-up and her large blue eyes, her best feature, are accentuated artfully. Marlene certainly doesn't look our age and is known for her honesty. She proudly shares her motto: Anyone can stay young with the help of the right plastic surgeon.

"I liked the book also. I wasn't surprised by the ending. I figured out who did it, but I thought it was a good mystery, since it kept you guessing pretty much throughout the whole book." She shrugged.

"Of course you knew who the murderer was. All you do is read those murder mysteries," Frances says with a laugh, and everyone else joins in except Ella.

"Okay Ella, it's your turn," I say to the plain-looking woman on my right. She is of medium height, medium weight, wears no make-up and pulls her gray hair back in a ponytail. She wears a nice pair of navy blue slacks and a plain, pale blue sweater, but both are at least two sizes too big. All of her clothes are baggy. Ella and her husband owned our neighborhood grocery store until a huge supermarket opened up across the street and drove them out of business. Her husband never was the same. Ella went to work for the school district, but he never seemed to be able to hold down a job more than a year or two after that.

"I didn't like the book," she states emphatically. "I didn't like the fact that that woman was the murderer."

The other two women at the table groan and cover their faces in their hands.

"You never like the books. Who should have been the murderer if not that woman, Ella?" Frances asks patiently.

"I don't know, maybe the detective," Ella answers uncertainly.

"The detective wasn't even in the story until after the murder. The sister-in-law could have done it, though," supplies Marlene, attempting to be helpful.

"I didn't think she could have done it either," Ella says.

"It seems you haven't liked any of the books we've read in a couple of years," Frances says calmly.

"I liked that one about the woman who lived by the lake. Remember that one?" Ella says enthusiastically.

"That's only because you liked the dog," Marlene states. "And *Where the Crawdads Sing*. You only recommended that book because Delia Owen was in her seventies when she wrote it."

"Well, we should support older women," Ella states with enthusiasm.

"But did you like the book?" I ask earnestly.

"I don't remember."

Marlene, annoyed, says, "Then why do you even belong to the book club?"

"Now, wait a minute," I say seriously. "She's entitled to her opinion, even if she disagrees with all of us."

"I can't help it if I'm more conservative than the rest of you. Everyone enjoyed the last novel I recommended, didn't you?" Ella asks anxiously.

"Yes, we did. But I don't want to read Christian romance novels all the time. Once in a while is fine, Ella. But you nix most mysteries and science fiction, since you want no violence at all. And worst of all, no sex! Honey, that's the only excitement girls our age can get," Marlene complains, and Frances and I laugh.

"You can opt out of any book you don't approve of and that's fine, but you can't censor all of our books. Okay?" I ask, and Ella nods.

"In fact, I need to talk to Anthony about our waiter," Marlene continues.

"What's wrong with Sam? He's taking excellent care of us like he has for years," I point out, confused.

"That's just it! I've enjoyed flirting with him for years. But then he went and got married. You know I don't make passes at married men. I'll have to ask Anthony if he can assign a single server to us from now on," Marlene smiles.

"Don't you dare!" Ella yelps, horrified.

"She's only kidding," I tell Ella as I try to control my laughter. "After all these years, you still can't tell when she's trying to shock us." Frances and I breathe a sigh of relief when Ella laughs, too.

"What about you Millie? What did you think of the book?" Frances asks.

"Oh, I really enjoyed it. For a while there I thought it was a toss-up between the sister-in-law and her husband. But the wife messed up when she mentioned the briefcase," I point out.

"I completely missed that, Millie," Frances laughs. "By the way, that green blouse really matches your eyes. Is it new?"

"Yes, I got it on sale at Cora's Dress Shop," I tell them.

"Have you ever thought of dying your hair its original color?" Marlene asks me.

We all burst out laughing.

"I don't think my family would appreciate their eighty-five-year-old grandmother running around with bright red hair," I chuckle.

"It really was red, wasn't it?" Frances covers her lips with her hands as we all continue to giggle.

"Okay, folks," I say. "Enough of this. Shall we discuss the book for next month? I suggest we consider a classic."

"Please, no Shakespeare!" Frances says, her fingers entwined as if she's praying. "After trying to explain him to a class of twenty-four teenagers every year, I made a vow I'd never read him again."

"Fine, no Shakespeare," I say. "We've read practically all of Hemingway's books. Any suggestions?"

"How about Faulkner?" Marlene chimes in. "Years ago, I watched a movie called *The Reivers,* it was based on the last book Faulkner wrote before he died. It won a Pulitzer Prize a year after. It was really a good movie, and Steve McQueen starred in it. I thought it was one of his best films. And he is oh-so easy on the eyes." She bats her eyelashes and smiles.

"Well, I like Steve McQueen, too. Why don't we just watch the movie?" Frances says, and we all giggle.

"How about *The House of the Seven Gables?"* I say. "One year Harry and I did a Fall Foliage Trip up in New England and visited Salem. Since we had both read the book in high school, we decided to take the guided tour through the actual home that's in the book. It was really exciting."

"Why didn't we read that book years ago? Then we could have taken a side trip to Salem and visited the actual house, *before* I was on this damn walker." Ella laughs, and we all join in. It's nice to finally see her enjoying herself. She's had a hard year. We've all lost our husbands too, and we understand what she's going through.

"Any other suggestions?" Everyone shakes their heads so I say, "Okay, next month's book is *The House of the Seven Gables.*"

I turn to Fran and say, "Are you okay? You seem a little distracted tonight."

"They found a lump on my daughter-in-law's mammogram," Frances answers with a worried look in her eyes.

"Are they doing a biopsy?" I ask.

"Yes. The doctor says it's really small and there's nothing to worry about. But we've all heard that before, haven't we? Plus, you know the statistics. Black women have a forty percent higher death rate from breast cancer," Frances responds.

"Fran, you don't even have a diagnosis yet," I say. "Remember, last year my lump was benign. When *we* were young, breast cancer was a death sentence, but nowadays, the survival rate improves every year. And not every form of breast cancer is fatal. The surgeon I worked for—breast cancer was his specialty. Many of his patients were African American. Year after year, so many women would come back for checkups without any recurrence. Plus, your daughter-in-law lives an hour away from one of the top five cancer hospitals in the country. She's got a lot in her favor, and I'll also add her to my church's prayer list."

"We'll all pray for her," Ella promises.

Marlene shakes her head as we all reach around the table, joining hands for a quick squeeze.

"I'm gonna check on Netflix tomorrow," Marlene says, "and see if I can get that movie with Steve McQueen. If I can, why don't we do a movie night next Friday at my house, say six o'clock?"

"That sounds great!" Ella says. "I'll bring some brownies."

"Oh good, and I'll bring the vanilla ice cream," Frances laughs.

"And I'll bring pizza," I add.

"Sounds like a date, then!" Marlene says, laughing too.

"Should I call for an Uber now?" I ask everyone.

"Not for me." Marlene says. "My son is picking me up. He's gonna spend the night tonight."

"Oh, that's nice," Ella says.

"Not really. I think he's coming to give me a lecture. He's probably worried about his inheritance. Remember, I'm going on that cruise with the women from church, and he hates when I spend money. Plus, he's afraid I might meet a man on the boat and get married again."

Marlene has married very well, twice, and has often said she's open to husband number three.

"I think on my way out," Marlene winks and continues, "I'll flirt with one of the waiters in front of my son, make him nervous. Oh, there he is in the foyer. See you all on Friday!" She laughs as she leaves.

I watch her walk away in her brown wool, tailored slacks that hug her hips and her burnt orange sweater that outlines her upper body. I'm convinced Pilates really do work as I observe two older men enjoying the view. I marvel at the fact that, at age seventy-eight, she still wears high heels.

"We never did discuss expanding the group," Frances says.

"I know," I say. "Maybe we should talk about it on Friday night. I wouldn't mind having one or two more members." I say.

"But what if they don't like us?" Ella says, sounding so insecure.

"What if we don't like them?" Frances laughs.

"You know when my son first joined the police department, he was on probation. Maybe we could put them on probation?" Ella says, giggling.

Frances and I burst out laughing.

"I've never heard of a book club where you're put on probation," I say, enjoying Ella's joke. "And besides, how would we ever explain Marlene?"

Nick

It's crowded tonight, in spite of the weather. Saturday night—the best night of the week! The customers waiting for tables are three-deep at the bar. Tips will be great! During the week, the bar is usually empty, and all I do is fill drinks for the restaurant. Me, I live for the crowd. I'm a great bartender—organized, efficient, and I always remember what my customers are drinking. And I can read people. Do they want to be left alone, do they want to talk or just need me to listen?

Evenings like this, though, reinforce my decision to look for a new job. I need to work where there's more action, like a singles bar, surrounded by great-looking women. After all, I'm a good-looking guy. Since I was fifteen, I've watched how women looked at me, reacted to my smile. They say it's my black hair and blue eyes. One gal said I have "black Irish" good looks, whatever the hell that means. I just know that I've always scored with the ladies. I guess you might say I'm conceited, but I say I'm just honest.

Tony's has a high-class, sophisticated atmosphere. The bar has an old-world feel—high gloss, dark mahogany with brass fixtures. The barstools are barrel shaped, with thick padding and covered in soft brown leather, designed to encourage customers to linger. Large bowls of mixed nuts and small cut-glass candleholders decorate its surface. Lighting and music are low. Crystal glasses are large; you get a generous drink at Tony's.

A six-foot, etched glass wall separates the bar from the front door, a good thing on a cold, rainy night like this. Every time the front door opens, the wind sends a chill over everyone in its vicinity.

The cute, new waitress, Kelly, comes to get her order.

"Hey doll, how's it going?" I ask. "Want to go out for coffee or something after work tonight?"

"I don't think so, I have a lot of studying to do," she answers.

She's been giving me the runaround, always making excuses. If she doesn't have to study, she has other plans. It's okay, though, I know she'll come around—they always do. In fact, tonight, I'll walk her to the bus stop and get her to change her mind.

I have been weighing my options lately. Tending bar is only temporary. During the day, I've been taking acting lessons, and as soon as I can afford it, I'm gonna add singing and dancing lessons too. I haven't told anyone, but I have an agent now and he's gotten me several auditions. So far, I've only landed a few bit parts, nothing to brag about—yet. My big break is coming, though, I know it. Positive attitude is everything, just as important as talent, and maybe even more so. And I've got lots of attitude.

I hope I won't put Anthony in a bind when I quit. Anthony's okay—he's a good boss. He hired me when I was in a real financial bind, even took me on without any references. But that was two years ago, and it's time to move on. One night, a couple of months ago, when I couldn't sleep, I caught this old movie on TV, "Cocktail." My hero, Tom Cruise, played this bartender who could throw bottles up in the air, catch them behind his back and pour drinks practically at the same time. It was really cool. Ever since then, I've been practicing and I'm getting really good. This fancy joint is too quiet. I need loud music, dancing, and lots of chicks—a singles bar like the Wild Flamingo downtown. I'd fit right in at a place like that.

Maybe I should consider changing locations instead of just jobs. Maybe it's time to move to New York, try to get on Broadway. I might even find a nice rich woman there who'll set me up, take care of me, a nice sugar mama. I could handle that. Or California might be better, try for a movie role. At least it's warm there and I could room with my old buddy, Ray.

Most of our customers are older. I need young people, like that chick in the tight red dress, a little flashy but hot as hell. Better yet, the classy, good-looking redhead who came in a little while ago. She's gorgeous, way out of my league, but given the opportunity, I'd take a run at her. What the hell she's doing with that old fart, I'll never know. Yeah, right, of course I know: money. When I make it big, I'll have chicks like her hanging all over me.

I never intended to be a bartender. One Fourth of July, when I was a kid, my mom and I snuck out of the house, and left my dad drunk and sound asleep on the couch. We went into town to watch the parade and later on, the fireworks. It was only when we got there that we heard that the city had arranged a flyover by the Blue Angels. I was about twelve at the time and I can remember my excitement and the fear I felt while watching those planes, their wings so close, I was sure they were gonna crash. They flew sideways, upside down, and I kept forgetting to breathe. With their engines so loud and the crowd cheering, I couldn't hear a word my mom was saying. Afterward, I stood in line and got one of the pilots to sign a flier I picked up on the lawn in the park. I was so excited I told my mom I was going to be a pilot when I grew up.

Of course, by the time we got home, my dad was awake and yelling. He smacked my mom for taking me into town. As usual, he ruined everything. I couldn't even play Little League sports. My dad would never spend the money, but I used to go watch them work out. I'd go to the field late in the evening and copy what they did. I'd run the track, the bleachers and do whatever exercises they did. Over the years, as I got taller, my upper body began to develop.

One day, when I was almost fifteen, I'd had enough. My dad hit my mom, so I knocked him on his ass. I told him if he ever hit her again, I was gonna kill him. I never saw fear in my dad's eyes before then, but he never hit my mom again. I have to admit I scared myself that day. Until then, I'd been such a mild-mannered kid, but for the first time, I experienced true anger.

I made really good grades in school and I read every book in the school library about pilots and flying airplanes. When I started high school, I made an appointment with my counselor and asked what I had to do, what classes I had to take, to become a Blue Angel. I remember how she sat there staring at me with that shocked and sad look on her face.

"Nicholas, college is very expensive and you would need a degree in aviation from a really good school. Your grades are good, but I doubt you could get a full scholarship to the kind of school you would need to attend. Plus, I believe, they usually require that you have taken flying lessons. And with your situation at home…"

I didn't let her finish. I just got up and walked out of the room. What was I thinking? The only child of the town drunk would never be admitted to the Blue Angels. The counselor kept trying to talk to me, but I just ignored her.

To prove how wrong she was, I kept studying and made great grades. But she was right. I never made the grades that would earn me a full scholarship to a top ten school.

One day near the end of my senior year, Mrs. Wallace stopped me in the hall.

"I think I might have found a great alternative for you, Nicholas," she said, seeming genuinely excited. "But you have to come to my office tomorrow morning at ten AM sharp."

I have to admit I was curious, and agreed. But when I got home that night, I had another fight with my dad. My mom was sick again. She never was very healthy. But he refused to take her to the hospital. I was about to call my friend Jeff, and ask him to drive us to the emergency room when my mom pulled me aside. She promised we would go in the morning right after my dad left for work. I hardly slept at all that night.

In the morning, I found my dad sitting at the kitchen table, crying. He told me that during the night, my mom had died in her sleep. He said he had called the police and they were on their way. I went into their bedroom. Mom finally looked at peace.

I kissed her goodbye, went into my bedroom and packed my things, including the envelope of money Mom said she was saving for my graduation present. She had asked me to hide it for her.

I walked back into the kitchen and punched my dad in the face. The rage I felt as I stood looking down at him as he held his broken nose, blood staining his t-shirt, was something I never wanted to feel again. I turned, walked through the living room, and out the front door. I've never regretted leaving and I've never been back. I'm afraid if I had stayed, I would have been tempted to do more than just break his nose.

I will admit I've watched that movie *Top Gun* many times, and if I ever do get to Hollywood, I'm going to try to meet Tom Cruise. I want to ask him what it really feels like to fly one of those jet planes.

One of the waiters interrupted my reminiscing. "Hey Nick, what was the commotion down the street earlier? Lots of police cars. Something big must have gone down."

"Probably a drunk driver, but don't worry, he didn't get over-served here," I answer.

I watch the number of drinks my customers order. Our town has started prosecuting bartenders for serving drunks. I'll have to watch that at those single bars. That's all I need—trouble with the law.

It's kind of ironic, me ending up a bartender. Customers are always offering to buy me drinks, which I always refuse. *Can't get drunk on the job, you know.* I wonder what they'd think if they knew that I don't drink. That I've never consumed a single drop of alcohol in my whole life.

That's one thing my old man taught me: my body is a temple. No way I'm gonna end up a falling down drunk like him. I only hung around as long as I did to protect my mom. The old bastard was a mean drunk and didn't stop beating on her until that day I showed him I could protect her. I don't even know if he's dead or alive and could not care less. Me, I avoid anything addictive—no alcohol, no drugs, no tobacco, not even caffeine.

I guess that's why I've never been able to settle down and get married. I find a girl I really like and I get nervous. After a couple of dates, if she gets a little tipsy, or starts acting like a party girl, it's time for me to move on. I've lived with one alcoholic. I could never do that again. It's also hard to find a girl who's willing to follow my fitness regimen. Or maybe it's me. Maybe I just like playing the field and use that as an excuse.

I'll have to visit a shrink when I'm rich and famous. Maybe he can help me find out why I do what I do. Is it my past or my present lifestyle that's the problem?

But one thing I know for sure, thanks to my dad, I'll never lay a hand on a woman. Any man who does is no man, as far as I'm concerned. I've gotten in trouble more than once, interfering in situations like that, stepping in and saying, "Hey big man, you want to fight? Instead of picking on a woman, why don't you try a fair fight for a change?"

Ended up with several black eyes and lots of sore knuckles.

The blonde sitting at the end of the bar is a real looker. She's been giving me the eye all night and she seems to be alone. Oh well, maybe I'll blow Kelly off and make a move on the blonde. You gotta be flexible. I think I'll flash my signature smile, stroll down the length of the bar and turn on the charm.

Alison

THE WAITER LEADS US TO THE MOST OBSCURE CORNER OF THE RESTAURANT. We have come bearing the most unwanted gift: a small child. I place my son in the corner and shield him from the view of other patrons. My husband sits across from me, excited about this evening.

"This is a special occasion. It's Mommy's birthday and I think you're old enough to eat at a fancy restaurant. Don't you?"

Paul smiles at his dad.

This is not my idea. I am a mother. I've taken my son to places I shouldn't have, and I've paid the price in aggravation and embarrassment—the wrong dress shop, lunch with my single friends. I've learned this lesson. I've paid my dues.

I look at Paul. He looks so grown up in his little suit and a tie, just like his dad's. His golden hair is neatly combed, his big blue eyes scanning his surroundings. How could he be almost five years old? How fast these years have gone by! I realize he's not my baby anymore. He's a little boy. In the spring, he starts kindergarten and both our lives will change forever. He has a sunny personality, is quick to laugh with a lively curiosity; he is the joy of my life.

He starts to swing his feet, loudly kicking the legs of the chair in the process. He pulls on his tie.

"Stop that!" his dad says. "In a restaurant, you sit still. Don't fidget, it's not polite. Big boys don't do that."

Paul turns his questioning eyes to me. I smile reassuringly and say, "You look like such a big boy today. You look just like Daddy."

"I know, we look like twins," Paul giggles.

I giggle, too. I'm determined to protect my son tonight. This trip will probably end in disaster. But it's not his fault that I couldn't make his father understand. I won't let Paul get hurt during this trip. Children aren't the only ones who have to learn life lessons. Sometimes dads have to learn them also, and I'll shield my son from the inevitable wrath.

Now Paul begins to hum and squirm. He picks up his spoon and begins to tap the table with it.

Doug glares at him and says, "Stop that."

Paul stops.

It's interesting that the things that bring me the most joy tend to bring his father such annoyance. It isn't that Doug doesn't love him as much as I do; it's that he doesn't understand him. Doug is an only child, growing up in a lonely, quiet environment, raised by older, stricter parents. I remember when I first met my in-laws, how structured they were. I tried to help his mom in the kitchen, but she very sweetly refused my offer. Everything in the refrigerator and the cabinets had a designated place and she was afraid I might put something in the wrong place.

When Paul came along, they were excited about their new grandchild. But whenever we would visit, it turned into such a chore. We had to bring a portable crib, the baby swing, baby seat and all his other supplies. And the older he got, the harder our visits became.

They refused to put up their precious glassware to accommodate a toddler. I had to follow him around everywhere. I was a nervous wreck, fearing that he might break something. They never were comfortable with baby Paul.

It wasn't until the last two years that they have offered to babysit him, asking if he could spend the night. It's like they were waiting for Paul to become a full-grown child before they wanted a relationship with him. And there are always rules at Grandma and Grandpa Morgan's house. No food except in the kitchen. And when he wants a cookie, he has to kneel on a chair at the kitchen table and lean over as far as possible. Then he hopefully won't get any crumbs on the floor. I'm exhausted by the time we head for home.

I, on the other hand, am from a large, noisy family that loves children. All of our homes are toddler proofed. We enjoy the innocent behavior of young children and are more tolerant. When we are all together, the children run and play, and the noise level can be deafening. I watch my son do things my nieces and nephews have done before, and I enjoy the comparison. And children in my mom's house can eat a cookie in the living room.

When I announced I was pregnant, my parents immediately purchased a new crib and swing for their spare room to replace the older ones from previous grandchildren. They stocked the room with diapers and everything else a new baby requires. Whenever we visited, all I needed to bring was a diaper bag. They were totally prepared for his arrival and completely relaxed around him.

Whenever Doug and I have needed a babysitter, my parents always are the first to volunteer. And when Paul is there, I know he can play with his cousins or by himself and I don't have to worry that he's causing my parents any problems. Paul loves Doug's parents, but I don't know if he'll ever be as close to them as he is to mine.

Doug often asks, "Why can't we have a little peace and quiet around here?"

How do I explain that we missed that boat about four years ago?

Doug begins his lesson by saying, "We got all dressed up today because it's Mommy's birthday and it's a special day, just like your birthday."

"Will she get a Scooby Doo cake too?" Paul asks, wide-eyed.

"No, but we get to eat really great food and Mommy doesn't have to cook."

Food: that's another problem. Tony's obviously doesn't cater to children; it's an adult restaurant, not a family friendly place. I imagine ordering two peanut butter and jelly sandwiches so my son will feel more comfortable here. I may go ahead and try, but that would probably infuriate my husband.

I often feel that children are like small steam engines – needing motion to release the energy building up inside. My son, proving my theory, begins to wiggle in his seat, and I smile. He smiles back with so much love in his eyes, my heart contracts.

He slowly picks up his napkin. My husband sends me a gloating look that says, *See, I told you he was old enough to eat here.* I watch as Paul slowly shakes it out and puts it on his head. I laugh, and my husband frowns.

Doug starts another lecture on manners, saying, "It's not good manners to do that, Paul. We don't sing—we use our inside voice, and we don't run or jump."

Paul stares at his dad and tries to understand what he's done wrong. Patiently, he listens to his dad's long explanation of restaurant rules. He longingly looks out the window and sighs, then says, "But I thought we were going to McDonald's."

I laugh and smile at my husband. He scowls back. I see the moment resignation sets in. My husband accepts his defeat gracefully and smiles back.

"I only wanted…" he starts.

"I know," I interrupt. "I've been there. Remember when I took him out to lunch with Ronnie and Candy from college and he knocked over the pitcher of iced tea? And just imagine what it's going to be like when we have two."

"Yeah," Doug replies.

I sit smiling, waiting for what I have just said to sink in.

"…Two of what?" he asks, looking so suspicious.

Now I am really laughing. "Well, I'm not talking about buying two kittens, if that helps you figure it out."

Doug looks so happy and excited; I have to keep myself from jumping out of my chair and throwing myself into his arms. He reaches across the table, grabs both my hands and squeezes them. He leans forward, kisses my fingertips, and knocks his water glass over.

Doug looks horrified and we begin sopping up the mess with our napkins. I am trying so hard not to laugh.

"Oh no!" I hear Paul gasp. "Is Daddy in trouble?"

"No, honey. It was an accident. Everything is fine." I smile and run my fingers through his golden hair to reassure him.

"Are you sure?" Doug asks.

"Of course, I'm sure." I giggle.

"Are we buying a kitten?" Paul asks, all excited.

"Maybe. Would you like to buy a kitten or a puppy, honey?" I ask him.

"I think a kitten and a puppy, Mommy. Could we buy both?" Paul is getting too excited.

"We'll talk about it later. Okay?" I run my fingers through his hair again and try to calm him down.

"We need to celebrate." Doug is talking so fast. "Should I order champagne? Oh no. No alcohol, right? I'm so excited, I'm not even thinking straight. I can't wait to call my mom; she's been asking me when we were going to have another one for the last two years."

"Really? You never told me that." I have to admit, I'm surprised.

"I didn't want to put any more pressure on us then we already had. You didn't need your mother-in-law on your back while we were trying so hard to get pregnant!" he explains.

"I always thought they felt we shouldn't have another child," I say.

"Well in the beginning, I think that was true. But they grew to love Paul so much. And the more time they spent around your family, they started to realize how much they missed by not being more involved with Paul when he was a baby. My mom recently told me, she learned a lot from watching your mother and the way she treats all her grandchildren. She said they never offered to take care of the baby because they felt we thought they were too old. And then the last two summers, when we started spending a week at the beach house with your parents, they felt left out and, to be honest, a little jealous of our relationship with your parents. I think they regret how they acted in the past."

I feel bad that Doug hasn't shared any of this with me.

"Doug, you know I love your mom and dad. I never mean for them to feel left out. It's just that the beach house is mobbed when we're all there. You know how big my family is, how loud it can get, and how structured your parents are. I really felt it would be too chaotic for your folks to even stop by for the day. But now, I feel awful."

"Don't feel bad," he says. "When I call them, they'll be so happy to hear the news. Now that we know, we can take care of it this summer. I think they'd love it if I drove them out to the beach house for the day. But I feel, right now, we should at least order dessert or something."

"What I'd really like to do is just leave," I say with a smile. "No one will notice or care, for that matter. It's Saturday night, they'll probably be grateful for the table."

"How about we come back next Saturday?" Doug says.

"I'd love that."

"Do we have to?" Paul whines.

"No sweetheart. You could stay with Grandma Opal if you'd like," I tell him.

"Okay!" He smiles.

Doug throws some bills on the table and we start the long walk to the front door. Doug walks ahead, pulling Paul behind him. I follow, watching my son smile and wave to the patrons. Most people understand, smile and wave back. Some send disapproving glances.

Doug must have noticed because he picks up his son and places his arms around him, guarding him from any censure. He loves his son fiercely and will always try to keep him safe.

As we near the exit, Paul, facing the restaurant over Doug's shoulder, shouts, "We're going to McDonald's!"

Several of the customers laugh, and a few even clap.

Doug grabs my hand and leans closer. "This has been the greatest night ever, and I love you both so much."

I smile and squeeze his hand. Together we run laughing through the rain, headed for the Golden Arches.

Rickie

My uncle looks surprised and suspicious when I hurry in out of the rain and walk through the front door of the restaurant.

Liam, one of our new waiters, holds out his hand and says, "Here, let me take your jacket, Rickie. I'll hang it up in back, over by our lockers. It will probably dry off by the time you leave." He smiles.

"Thanks, Liam, I appreciate that," I laugh.

"Hi, Uncle Louis. How're you doing?" I say as I walk over toward his lectern, running my hands through my wet hair, still smiling.

"Fine, Rickie. Fine. How about you? Is anything wrong?" he asks, frowning.

"No. Why would you think something's wrong?" I ask.

"Well, you never stop by like this, especially on a Saturday night." He looks concerned.

Tony's Restaurant is like a second home to me. I've been in and out of here all the time since I was a baby. But my uncle is right. I don't think I've ever just stopped by on a weekend night.

"Well, yeah, I guess you're right," I chuckle. "But I need to talk to my dad, if he's available."

"He's busy at the moment. He's in his office, on the phone with one of our new vendors out in California. He'll probably be a while."

"If it's okay with you, I'll wait." I shift my weight from one foot to the other.

"You seem nervous. Are you okay?" he asks.

"I'm fine." I smile and freeze my lips for as long as I can.

Louis turns away to greet two customers, rattles off his usual spiel and leads them to their table. I am always amazed at how pleasant and friendly he remains, no matter how busy things get at the restaurant or how many hours he works.

I look out the window and watch the rain pound the sidewalk out front with almost as much force as the small power washer my dad purchased for the house.

My uncle returns to his station and I turn to face him.

"So how are your grades?" he asks. "Are you still on the honor roll?"

"Yes, I am, Uncle Louis," I answer, patiently.

"Still taking all advanced classes?"

"Yes, and we're not gonna play twenty questions until my dad gets off the phone. This is a private conversation I need to have with him." I try to be as tactful as possible.

"Okay, okay. Didn't mean to stick my nose where it doesn't belong."

Moving to stand next to my uncle, I place my hand on his shoulder and say earnestly, "Now don't go getting your feelings hurt. As soon as I talk to my dad, I'll fill you in on everything, okay?"

Another waiter, Darrell, waves to me as he approaches. He explains to my uncle that they have run out of red wine. My uncle asks me to answer the phone until he comes back and hurriedly takes off, headed for the storage closet.

Standing behind the lectern, I realize this is the only job in the restaurant I haven't worked. I started out unloading trucks before I was old enough to work inside and was promoted to washing dishes. I even spent time in the kitchen chopping vegetables before I graduated to busboy and then waiter. My dad believed his dad had the right idea: we should learn the business from the bottom up.

Uncle Louis is back and I'm happy to step aside. Thankfully, the phone only rang once, and it was a wrong number.

"What are you gonna do about the wine? I ask. I know what a catastrophe it can be if you run out of any supplies.

"Nothing," my uncle laughs. "I found two boxes over in the corner. How did you make out?"

"Fine. Darrell must have alerted the staff. A few people arrived and fortunately they all had reservations. A couple of waiters took them to their tables immediately. There was this one couple, though. They had a little boy and they left before they ordered any food."

"Were they upset?" My uncle looks concerned.

"I asked them if there was a problem and they said that everything was fine. They were laughing and looked really happy," I say, shrugging my shoulders.

"Well, as long as they were happy. You know, Rickie, if you need me to run interference for you, I will. It won't be the first time. I've done that before." My uncle smiles.

"Why would I need you to run interference?" I ask, frowning.

"Well, maybe you're in trouble?" My uncle asks seriously.

"What kind of trouble? I'm eighteen, never been a problem my whole life," I say, a bit too defensively. Oh, how I wish my dad would get off the phone. I am nervous enough without having to deal with my uncle, too.

"I know that. But a lot of good kids get into trouble, and that's why parents and uncles worry."

Louis pauses to answer the phone, and once more I'm impressed with the friendly way he answers questions.

Once I have his attention again, I say, "Uncle Louis, when I'm not home studying or doing my homework, I'm either at football practice or it's game night. I don't have time to get into trouble."

"Yeah, I know. But I also know you've started dating and you wouldn't be the first guy in high school to get a girl pregnant."

"Oh, good God." I lower my voice. I feel my blood start to boil and know I have to control my temper. "Are you crazy? Jeannie is a nice girl and she's as serious about her education as I am. And she's really smart. She just got accepted at Stanford." I try to modulate my voice. I hate when Louis interferes in my life.

"Isn't that school far away?" His eyes narrow.

"Yes, it's in California." I answer calmy.

"So, you're here to tell your dad you're planning to go with her to Stanford? He's not gonna like that." He shakes his head and scowls.

"No, Uncle Louis, that's not why I'm here." I clench my jaws.

"Why don't you go home. Relax. I'll have your dad call you and you can discuss this on the phone."

"Oh, that sounds like a great idea, Uncle Louis, but that's exactly why I'm here. I called my dad to tell him I had just gotten accepted to the university of *my* choice and do you know what happened?" I ask, my face flushed.

"No." My uncle looks grim.

"He hung up on me. Would he hang up on you or Uncle Dominick or my mom?" I'm trying to keep my voice low, but he can see I'm angry.

"Probably not Dominick, maybe not me, but definitely not your mom." My uncle smiles.

"I agree, definitely not my mom." I shake my head, calming down a little.

"But you're different—you're his kid."

"No, don't you see? I'm not a kid anymore. I graduate in a month and a half and then I'm leaving for the university. All of you expect me to act like an adult when I get there. He has to start treating me like one." I want my uncle to understand how I feel.

"What university did you get into?"

"Cornell." I answer solemnly.

"Isn't that where your Uncle Dominick went?" my uncle asks, his face hardening.

I nod my head.

"No wonder he hung up on you. I didn't know you wanted to be a lawyer." My uncle looks so sad I could cry.

"That's just it. I don't, and he wouldn't let me explain. You know how he can get. That's why I'm here."

"I don't remember your folks taking you to visit Cornell."

"Dominick did, while my parents were in New York at that convention," I explain.

'Oh, jeez, Rickie! He must feel so betrayed." My uncle stares at me like I am some kind of traitor. I can see the disappointment in his eyes.

At this point, I wonder if I should have waited until my dad came home later tonight. Once I explained everything to my mom, though, she understood. At least she would be an ally, unlike my Uncle Louis.

"Okay," he sighs. "So, when am I going to see you again, at Thanksgiving dinner?"

"Thanksgiving," I nod. "But you're also gonna see me tomorrow. I'm working the DeMarco anniversary party. Dad says they've reserved over half of the restaurant. It's their grandparents' seventieth wedding anniversary and you're expecting a big crowd. Dad said it's all hands-on-deck. You know I always help out at big events. That's if he's still taking to me." I smile a half-smile.

"That's great. Oh, look—your dad's off the phone," my uncle says, looking nervous. "Good luck."

"Don't warn him I'm headed back there," I say, pointing my finger at him.

"I won't, but don't forget to knock."

I glare at him and head toward my dad's office. I acknowledge each member of the staff that recognizes me with a smile and a wave.

I open the door and enter my dad's office.

"Didn't your mother teach you to knock before you enter a room?" my dad asks, annoyed.

"Didn't your mother teach you not to hang up on people?" I respond, equally annoyed.

I see a flash of anger in his dark eyes, but I don't care.

"Look, Dad, we can discuss this like two adults or we can have a knock down, drag out fight. I'm okay either way," I say, then raise my voice. "And Uncle Louis, I know you're listening at the door. This is between me and my dad, so get lost."

"Louis, what are you doing out there?" My dad shouts.

"I came to tell you to keep it down. You two yelling back here will be bad for the staff's morale," Louis yells back.

"Is it bad for your morale too, Louis?" my dad asks, his voice still loud.

"Anthony, how many times have you told me? I'm not staff; I'm family."

"Well then, Louis, lock the door so no one comes back here."

My dad and I look at each other and smile. Then he says to me, "Sit."

"Will you listen to me, no interruptions?" I ask. I point to the small refrigerator next to my dad's desk. "Is it okay if I grab a Coke?"

He bobs his head up and down.

I take a huge gulp and begin. "Uncle Dominick was waiting for me after practice one day. We went for coffee and he told me that the Alumni Association at Cornell offers yearly scholarships, anywhere from three full scholarships to several partial ones. He wanted to talk to you about submitting my name to take the test. I asked, since I would be eighteen then, if I could take it without your permission. Uncle Dominick asked why. I explained that I didn't want to get your hopes up, in case I failed. I had been offered a few smaller scholarships and we hadn't even discussed Cornell. The test was the weekend you and Mom went to that convention. I took the test and Uncle Dominick showed me around the campus."

I take a few sips of Coke and continue, "I got the letter today, Dad. I got a full scholarship—tuition, room, board, even books and labs. Can you believe it? I never wanted to be a lawyer. I considered Cornell for two reasons. First, it has one of the best business schools in the nation, and second, because it's closer to home. My plan always was to work with you here at the restaurant."

Another sip, and I cough when it goes down the wrong way. Then I say, "The only problem is, when I told Carmen, she had a fit. She said I'm stealing her dream. She insists she's always been the one who was going to take over after you retired. She's even researching colleges that have restaurant management programs. So, it looks like before you retire, we're going to need a business model with an eye towards expansion. In the future, I can see two Tony's, one on each side of the city."

I look at my dad and see tears in his eyes.

"I guess I owe you an apology," he says. "I always felt you were interested in the business; it never crossed my mind you might want something else. And then I thought Dominick had gone behind my back. I guess I owe Dominick a giant thank you. I'm so proud of you, Rickie! A full scholarship. Wow. Wait until your mother hears." Then he chuckles and says, "What am I saying? She probably already knows, right?"

"Yeah, she does. When she read the return address, she demanded to know what was going on. There's no way to keep things from Mom."

"Well, you better get home. I've got to get back to work. We're busy tonight," he says, walking around his desk.

"I love you, Dad." I stand up and give him a big hug.

"I love you too, son."

As I'm heading for the front door, Uncle Louis catches up with me.

"Everything okay now?" he asks, smiling and looking almost giddy.

"Yep, everything is fine. I'll call you later on tonight."

"That's okay. Congratulations. A full scholarship, no less. I can't wait to tell the staff." My uncle laughs.

"I don't need to call you, do I? You heard every word, didn't you?" I walk outside, smiling and standing a lot taller than when I came in.

Rachael

I RUSH IN OUT OF THE RAIN AND CHECK MY COAT. I'M GLAD I WORE THE raincoat with a hood. At least my hair isn't plastered to my head. I stop at the mirror by the front door for a quick check of the damages and fluff my short, curly black hair. I really should hit the ladies' room, refresh my makeup, but I'm already late. I hate to be late. I'm wearing my favorite royal blue dress, the one people say brings out the color of my eyes, and classic gold jewelry. How the hell did I let Matthew talk me into this—a blind date, at my age, no less?

"A college buddy of mine is in town this weekend, and I'll be gone on a business trip. Please, Rach! Please have dinner with him," he pleaded.

Oh well, I might as well get this over with. I've always wanted to try Tony's, and I wonder if Matthew picked it as a reward.

I weave my way through the crowded bar, looking for Matthew's friend. No tall, dark, handsome man wearing a red tie. I scan the dining area. Well, there he is, sitting at a table right in the middle of the room. Matthew got the handsome part right, and his tie is definitely red.

I hurry over and sit down, saying, "You must be Jack. I'm Rachael, and I'm sorry I'm so late. I got stuck in traffic. Between the rain and it being Saturday, the roads can be crowded at this time of night. Matthew and I have been friends for years. He told me you would be in town for a few days. And he said to say how sorry he was that he's out of town and missed you. First thing we should get straight is, I'm not very good at this. I've never been on a blind date before, so I really don't know the parameters."

He smiles and says, "I guess the first rule is, you order a drink." He indicates the pretty young waitress standing by the table.

I laugh, apologize to the young woman and order a glass of white wine.

"The next thing I should point out," I say, "is that when I'm nervous, I tend to babble. So, at any time, feel free to tell me to stop talking. It can be embarrassing, but basically, you're stuck with me thanks to Matthew. Well for tonight, anyhow." I laugh, run my fingers through my short hair and bite the inside of my lip. I must look like a nervous wreck.

He smiles again but says nothing. I wonder if he is the strong, silent type or if I've just rendered him speechless. We study our menus, and I discreetly check him out. He has a great smile, rugged good looks and dark, brown eyes with thick, long eyelashes any girl would kill for.

"I guess we should start with personal particulates," I say. "I'm thirty-two years old, a computer programmer who recently opened my own business designing websites. I just signed a lucrative contract this afternoon, in fact. I really wanted to go out and celebrate my success tonight, but it was kind of hard to organize a group of friends on a Saturday night. But I was in a good mood when Matthew talked me into doing this. And I wasn't looking forward to staying home doing nothing. So, dinner at Tony's with a stranger sounded really interesting."

I take a deep breath and hope I haven't scared this poor man away.

"Well, I'm glad I was in town and could rescue you from a boring night at home alone. And I'm glad Matthew talked you into meeting a stranger for dinner. I owe him one." Jack laughs.

"Me too. How do you feel about animals? I love them, but I live in a small apartment so I don't have any. I don't think it's fair to keep them cooped up all day while I work." I smile.

Returning my smile, Jack responds, "I'm thirty-eight; love animals. I have an Irish setter. My house has a huge back yard, great for the dog. I travel a lot so the dog usually stays with a friend of mine while I'm gone. He also has a large piece of property so I know the dog is in good hands."

I say, "You're a lawyer, right? At least that's what Matthew said. He said you're with a firm in New York." I start to spin my wine glass around by the stem and hope I don't knock it over.

"Yeah, I am a lawyer, but I'm not with a firm anymore."

"I thought Matthew said you were." I frown.

"Well, I was, but like you, I now have my own business," he explains. "I started a little late building my own company. I spent three years in the Army, did two tours in Afghanistan. So, while I was working in New York, I was preparing, making plenty of contacts so that when I was ready to go out on my own, I was in a position to succeed."

"Oh, I see. What kind of business is it?" I ask.

"I'm a sports agent and I live in Seattle now."

"Seattle." I laugh. "Is the weather as bad as they say?"

"Not if you like rain. In fact, I feel right at home in your fair city tonight."

"A sports agent," I smile. "Represent anyone I know?"

"Perhaps. I don't know if you've ever heard of Jason Upton?" he asks.

"Oh. I'm impressed! Outfielder for the Seattle Mariners, Rookie of the Year, batting average 320, played in the all-star game, real up and comer; may be the next Willie Mays. Anyone else?"

"How about Bubba Whitehall, ever heard of him?" he asks, laughing.

"Wow, premier running back for the San Diego Chargers, three years in the Pro Bowl, free agent this year. It's a shame." I shake my head. "He really fits in with the Chargers' offense. Everybody's guessing who he'll sign with next."

"They'll know by tomorrow," he smiles.

"Really? Who did he go with? You can tell me. I won't tell anyone" I laugh and make a cross over my heart.

"It will be in the morning papers. He re-signed with the Chargers and I got him a really good deal. You sure know a lot about sports for a girl," he says, as if that's unusual.

"Mom presented my dad with three beautiful, bouncing baby girls. One was an amazing ballet dancer, one was a gifted writer, and one was a hopeless tomboy. My dad had been a semi-pro baseball player. So, he was an avid sports fan and was delighted that he got to teach his oldest daughter—me—everything he knew. My earliest memories were of attending every game that's played with a ball, a puck, or a shuttle. He never was into bocce, though." I smile and think—great personality, easy to talk to. Matthew certainly picked a winner.

He returns my smile. "Are your parents still in the picture?"

"No, we lost both of them a few years back. But I have my sisters. One lives in California and one in Vermont. We're spread out all over the country but we're still very close. How about you?" I ask.

"Only child; lost my dad two years ago. Mom divides her time between Seattle and Florida. When she's in Seattle, she spends most of her time with me, when she's not shopping and visiting her new friends. In Florida, she lives in a retirement village. I can't believe how active she is, swimming, doing water aerobics, book club, playing bridge. I have to keep her schedule straight so I don't call her on the wrong day. She and I are pretty close, though." He laughs. "Do you have a serious boyfriend; have you ever been married?"

"No to both. Started my career, didn't have time for any serious commitments. Too busy trying to get ahead, I guess. Well, I was engaged once, when I was in college," I laugh. "But that didn't last."

"Why not?" he asks, leaning forward and taking a sip of his beer.

"Well, it's hard to marry a guy when you find out he slept with your roommate." I frown.

"Before or after the engagement?" he asks, shaking his head.

"How about the week after? And you'll love his excuses. Turns out they came from the same hometown, which they forgot to mention. Dated in high school, even went to the prom together. But you see, it just happened. It wasn't anything serious. Why was I blowing it all out of proportion?"

I lower my head, cover my eyes with my hand and come up smiling. "Can you believe that?" I laugh.

"What a jerk." Jack says, shaking his head, too.

"I know. I was lucky I had Matthew and his partner Barry telling me I was doing the right thing when I refused to see him and just FedExed the ring back. How about you? Do you have any ex-fiancées you want to tell me about, horrible or otherwise?" I laugh.

"No. Same as you, I've been too busy building up my business. Nobody special in my life either, much to my mother's regret." He smiles.

"We both sound pretty boring, don't we?" I laugh. "Married to our jobs, I guess."

My salmon is excellent, the grilled vegetables crisp and crunchy, just the way I like them. He seems to be enjoying his steak. Tony's will definitely go on my list of places to take my clients.

"Do you like to travel?" I ask.

"Did some traveling with some buddies, but they all got married. And you?" he asks.

"Same thing. Seems we went from planning trips to planning baby showers. Haven't done much on my own. Mostly I spend my vacations visiting my sisters, playing with my nieces and nephews. I love kids," I say between bites of food.

"Me too. I got talked into coaching a Little League baseball team with a friend of mine. Get a real kick out of the little guys," he replies. "If you could go anywhere you wanted to, right now, where would you go?"

"Oh, I guess Hawaii or Alaska, maybe a cruise. Save the more exotic places for when the company is doing better and I could take more time off, more than just a week."

"I have a friend who went to Alaska, hiked out onto one of the glaciers. Says it was spectacular."

"With all this global warming, I guess that could be exciting, maybe even dangerous." I laugh.

The conversation flows effortlessly as the evening progresses. We discuss movies, music. We hit a few rough spots discussing literature, but nothing too radical. I can't seem to convince him that he should attend some poetry readings.

"Did you ever work for the C.I.A.?" he asks. "You already know my whole life story, my favorite book, even my favorite color."

We both laugh. "I told you I talk too much."

"I'm not complaining, just commenting." He smiles.

We decide to share a dessert and I cut the large piece of Tony's famous chocolate cake in half.

"I can't believe how you just cut that cake. Both pieces are exactly the same size," he says, amazed.

"I was the oldest of three girls. Cutting the cake was my job. If the pieces weren't even, my two younger sisters would argue over who got the larger slice. And I had to settle for the smallest piece. I guess I got good at it in self-defense. I guess it's a talent you never forget."

The moist chocolate cake, rich chocolate ganache and mocha filling are decadent.

Jack reaches across the table and takes my hand, saying "I'll be here until Wednesday. Since tomorrow is Sunday, would you consider spending the day with me, showing me around your fair city? And while we're at it, will you have dinner with me on Monday and Tuesday?"

"I'll have to check my busy schedule, of course, but the answer is yes," I say, a little breathless.

As we're about to exit the restaurant, he stops and says, "There's just one thing I have to tell you."

Oh no, here it comes, I think. *This is where he either tells me he's married or he's gay.*

He smiles and says, "My name isn't Jack, and I don't know who the hell Matthew is."

Danny

"Danny, what are we doing here?" Jill asks.

"Well, you always said this was the one restaurant you always wanted to go to, so I made reservations." I answer.

"But why tonight? It's not my birthday or yours. It's not the anniversary of when we started dating."

"You always say I'm not spontaneous enough, so I just picked a day—any day—and today was it. Is that a problem?" I respond.

"I just wish you had warned me. I would have worn something more appropriate, if I had known." She frowns.

"Are you kidding me? You look amazing. You're so beautiful. And that's one of my favorite dresses." I smile.

Jill is the type of woman who turns heads, mostly male heads. Tonight, she has on her knitted gray dress that accentuates all of her ample curves. Her jet-black hair is pulled back on both sides by a set of silver combs that matches the large earrings and necklace I brought back from a business trip to Mexico.

She sighs and rolls her chocolate brown eyes as she says, "They're all your favorite dresses. It's so discouraging. It doesn't matter if I'm wearing my slinky black dress or my cut-off jeans and a t-shirt, you always say the same thing. I look amazing, beautiful. It hardly seems worth bothering to get dressed up anymore. Do you see what I mean?"

"I guess not. So, from now on you want me to say you look awful, even if I think you look adorable?" I ask, smiling.

Jill sighs. "Take tonight, if I came out in my torn jeans and a t-shirt, would you have let me come to this restaurant dressed like that, or would you have told me to change?"

"That's a tough one. I love how your butt looks in those jeans," I laugh. "No seriously, I would have thought of something."

"Never mind." She sighs again.

I wonder when Jill started laughing less and sighing more. Sometimes I wonder if it's just Jill I don't understand or if all women are the same.

"Did you enjoy the food?" I ask. "I thought it was great."

"Yes, it was. I'd certainly recommend it." She admits begrudgingly.

"It was the best steak I ever had." I say enthusiastically.

"Danny, we have to talk," Jill says.

"Uh, oh. I don't like the sound of that," I laugh.

"The reason I wanted to stay at my house tonight was because I think we should stop seeing each other."

I am dumbfounded.

"Danny, don't just sit there. Say something." Jill says.

"Why?" I ask her.

"Why should you say something?" She blinks her beautiful, brown eyes.

"No, why should we stop seeing each other?" I try to stay calm.

"Oh, Danny. It's just that we do the same things over and over. We never go to any place new." She leans her elbows on the table and places her head in her right hand.

"What about tonight?" I ask, trying to understand what I've done wrong.

"We're only here because I complained. You never plan anything unexpected. You're so predictable. Our life is just so boring." She drops her left hand on the table and starts to tap her fingernails on the surface.

"Who is he?" I'm starting to get angry.

"What?" She looks so innocent.

"Who's the guy you're leaving me for, Jill?" Does she think I'm a fool?

"There is no other guy. How long have we been dating, almost two years? And we never go anywhere special." She complains.

"That's not true. Didn't we go on vacation to North Carolina this summer? Didn't we have a great time?" I am totally confused.

"That's a perfect example. You gave me two choices. We could go to Virginia or North Carolina. And when I chose North Carolina, you gave me three resorts to choose from. Now take my friend Theresa.

When she opened her birthday present from her boyfriend, he surprised her with two tickets to Hawaii." She holds her hands out to her sides, palms up, eyebrows raised, as if she's just proved her point.

"Isn't he the guy she found out was sleeping with her sister. Wow, I bet that was a surprise," I say, raising *my* eyebrows.

"Danny, cut it out. That's beside the point." She folds her hands on the table as if she's praying.

"No, Jill. That is exactly the point. I'm sure Theresa would gladly trade you her two tickets to Hawaii for a guy like me who wouldn't cheat on you for a million bucks."

"Amen to that," says the blond teenager at the next table who looks amazingly like an older Shirley Temple.

Jill swivels to glare at the kid and says, "Excuse me, but this is a personal conversation."

"Well excuse *me,* but you're talking rather loud," Blondie says.

Shirley's mother pulls her toward their table saying, "Kitty, behave yourself."

"I get it," I say to Jill. "What girl wants to spend her life with an engineer? The guy who takes care of her, repairs her car, fixes her dishwasher, her air-conditioning, thinks she's just as beautiful when she's in an evening gown as when she's sick in bed with the flu. The guy who tapes football games so he can watch her chick flicks with her instead. Oh, that guy. Who could blame you for not wanting him?"

I never believed in love at first sight until I was standing in line at Starbucks that day and saw the girl up ahead juggling her coffee container, laptop and purse. I could spot a disaster in the making. I stepped out of line and caught her earthbound computer just in time. Jill's shoulder length, black hair was in total disarray and being a man, it immediately brought to mind images of waking up in bed next to this gorgeous woman every morning for the rest of my life. However, her Hershey colored eyes were hostile, and she lunged forward to retrieve her laptop, thereby spilling her coffee all over my new shoes.

The look of horror on her face appealed to my weird sense of humor and I laughed and said, "So, this is how you reward Prince Charming when he tries to rescue a maiden in distress?"

She stopped, stared and broke into her amazing smile, and I thought I had found my happily ever after. But that was then, and this is now.

"Danny it's not..." she starts.

"Don't you dare say it's not me, it's you. Although I do agree. It *is* you. You don't recognize a great guy when he's sitting across the table."

The waiter approaches to ask if we would like dessert.

"Yes," I answer. "I'd like one of those giant cupcakes."

"Danny, I don't want any dessert," Jill says in that annoyed voice I'm so familiar with.

"I just want to leave."

"Well, Jill, leave whenever you like," I say, very businesslike. "You're a free woman. Me, I'm in the mood for one of Tony's famous cupcakes. Of course, you did arrive here with me and it's raining like hell out there, so you'll have to call a cab or hang around and wait."

"Danny, you don't even like sweets. Why are you doing this?" she asks, exasperated.

"Why do you care what I do? We're not a couple anymore, right?" I ask.

The waiter places the cupcake in front of me and asks if I want a cup of tea or coffee.

"This is not my cupcake," I tell the waiter. "Please take it back and get my cupcake."

The waiter looks confused and says, "Is there something wrong with the cupcake, sir?"

"Yes, my cupcake should have pink icing. I like pink icing; I ordered pink icing." I explain.

"Danny, what is the matter with you?" Jill whispers. "You didn't order pink icing, and now you're making a scene. Have you started taking drugs?"

"Me? Take drugs? Are you kidding? I'm far too boring to take drugs. And if I want to make a scene, I'll make a scene. This is the new Danny, the spontaneous Danny. The Danny who loves pink icing."

I turn to the waiter and loudly say, "Are you going to take this back or not? Never mind. Where's our usual waitress? Where is Kelly?"

"She's in the kitchen picking up a large order so I offered to take care of this table," he answers softly.

"Well, go tell her I need to talk to her *now,*" I say firmly.

"Danny, why are you acting like this? Just eat the damn cupcake so we can leave. This is embarrassing." Jill's head is rotating back and forth, trying to see if anyone is looking at us.

"You don't like boring. You don't even like spontaneous anymore, and now you don't like being embarrassed. Maybe what you're looking for is excitement. Maybe you'll get lucky and your next boyfriend will be a spy," I say smiling and shaking my head.

Kelly arrives and I point at the cupcake and say, "Kelly, this is not my cupcake. I ordered a pink cupcake."

She covers her mouth with her hand and says, "Oh my God, Danny. You did. I'll be right back." And she runs toward the kitchen.

Jill frowns and asks, "Do you know that waitress?"

"Yes, I met her when I stopped by to make our reservation," I inform her.

"You didn't just call to make a reservation?" Jill frowns.

"No. I wanted to make sure this place wouldn't disappoint you."

Everyone notices Kelly bringing my cupcake to our table, due to the giant sparkler in the middle. I wave her away from Jill and say, "That's not for her; it's mine. She just broke up with me."

Kelly is startled and almost teary-eyed. "Oh, Danny, I'm so sorry," she whispers.

"Better to know beforehand, don't you think? Hey, Kelly, do you have a boyfriend? Because I'm suddenly available. Would you like my phone number?" I ask.

"I would!" yells Kitty, the teenage eavesdropper.

"Would you mind your own business?" Jill shouts.

"Why? You don't want him, and in case you haven't noticed, he's a hunk." Kitty says.

Once again, Kitty's mother thankfully intervenes and yanks the teenager back around to her own table.

I shake my head, remove the sparkler and douse it in my water glass, exposing the two-carat diamond engagement ring.

"Oh my God, Danny. Did you buy that for me?" Jill cries.

"No, I bought it for the waitress," I sigh. "Of course, I bought it for you. But don't worry, I made sure it could be returned. You know how practical we engineers are."

"Oh, Danny! You never said anything about marriage. I waited and waited, but finally, decided I was wasting my time. That marriage just wasn't your thing." She pouts.

"What are you talking about? We looked at houses, furniture. We've even talked about children. Even though you always seemed to avoid those discussions."

"I figured when you realized I didn't want children, you'd never propose."

"You really don't want to have children, ever? I don't know, Jill. All the things you've said about me are true. I feel like you see that everyone is watching, so you'll say yes rather than be embarrassed. But I'm still just a boring engineer. You're probably right that we aren't right for each other," I say seriously.

I guess I'm really not that surprised when Jill stands up and marches away, headed for the front door. I think down deep, I've known for a quite a while that something was wrong. But I kept hoping that I could make Jill happy if only I found her a house and bought her a ring. I just hope she finds someone else who can succeed where I failed.

"So, Kelly, you never said if you're dating someone." I turn back to our waitress.

"No, I'm not. I'm too busy trying to get my degree," Kelly smiles.

"That's great. You're smart to get a degree. I know working and going to school is hard, but it will pay off big-time. Have you completed all your required math classes?"

"What? Why?" Kelly looks confused.

"Because I don't know if you overheard, but I'm an engineer and I also tutor math students at the local college. If you could ever use a little help, just give me a call. Algebra, geometry, calculus, trigonometry—you name it. I'm really good at it and think it's fun."

"Thanks, I'll keep that in mind," she laughs.

"You know what? I just realized I don't have anywhere to go for Thanksgiving dinner. I usually go with Jill to her family's house on the holidays," I say, trying to look sad.

"Well, you can come here. Tony's is open on Thanksgiving from three PM until seven. But if you're interested, you better make a reservation before you leave tonight."

"We'll be here," Kitty chimes in. "My family comes every year. And if you're not interested in me, my older sister is available, and she's gorgeous."

When Kitty's mother intervenes, Kitty says, "Okay, Mom. I'm just talking to my friends." She rolls her eyes and turns back to her table.

I look at Kelly and we burst out laughing.

"Will you be here Thanksgiving, Kelly?" I ask.

"Yes, but if I don't get back to work, I might be unemployed by then," she says, as she hands me my check.

"Here's my credit card *and* my business card in case you need a tutor.

Do you think we could go out for coffee after closing on Thanksgiving evening?"

"We'll see," Kelly says, taking my cards. She walks away, smiling.

I watch her head back to the kitchen and hope she's really lousy at math.

Kitty

THE MAÎTRE D' SHOWS US TO WHAT MY FATHER LAUGHINGLY CALLS "THE Jackson table." Our family has been coming to Tony's every Saturday night since I can remember. We celebrate birthdays, graduations, anniversaries—all our successes—here. Normal families gather around kitchen tables during a crisis; we head to Tony's. And tonight, my parents are facing a doozy. My older sister Lee Ann decided to marry her freaky boyfriend, Adair, and my parents are trying to talk her out of it. They even called for reinforcements. My older brother Gordon is supposed to make an appearance. Now that he is working on the other side of town, we don't see him as much as we used to.

Lee Ann is gorgeous—tall, big blue eyes, with wavy, long blond hair like the glamorous old movie stars, almost covering her right eye. How I wish I looked like her. Me, I'm described as petite and cute. People say I look exactly like a movie star, too—an almost-grown version of Shirley Temple. No matter what I do, I can't straighten this mass of curls on top of my head. And I don't know why God couldn't have gifted me with a few more inches of height and a portion of Lee Ann's ample bosom.

Why Lee Ann has settled for Adair, I'll never know. I have to admit he's good looking, but he's not the sharpest knife in the drawer, and he's been unemployed as long as she's known him.

I have to say, I don't usually agree with my folks all that much. But tonight, I'm on their side. As I watch Lee Ann lean back in her chair, arms crossed over her enviable chest, I know they are up against a brick wall this time.

The waiter comes and everyone orders their favorite meals, except me. I always try the chef's special. I love to experiment, which is one of the many things my mother dislikes about me. I see my mother roll her eyes, which means, "Why must you always be different?" without her having to say it out loud. But I don't mind, I like being different. It makes life interesting.

As we eat, I listen to my parents tag team Lee Ann. They're really good at it. Usually, they can wear you down if they keep it up long enough. But Lee Ann is holding her own. Of course, poor thing, she'll probably have indigestion before we leave the restaurant.

I really love Tony's. It's so intimate, and if I really concentrate, I can pick up pieces of conversations everywhere. You see, I'm a writer. Most people my age would say, "I'm going to be a writer." But I already am one. I graduate high school in June, and then in September I'm off to college to major in creative writing. I've been journaling since I was in fifth grade. I've entered writing competitions since junior high and have won several awards. I've read almost every "So You Want to Be a Writer" book in the school libraries. One book said good writers can pick up dialogue wherever they are, if they only pay attention. So I pay attention.

The owner's son, Rickie, just walked in. He's also a senior in my school but took all advanced classes so he could graduate in December. I wish I was like Lee Ann. She'd probably walk right up to him and say hi. My sister knows how to flirt. She's been trying to teach me, but I don't think it's working. Rickie waits tables at the restaurant during the summer and sometimes he talks to me. Once he said he thought my piece in the school paper that year was great, really funny. Of course, I was completely tongue tied and just blushed. Lee Ann kicked me under the table, but I couldn't think of anything to say.

Besides, Rickie has a girlfriend. She's smart and is graduating early too. I'm in advanced English. I'm smart enough to take all advanced classes, but I didn't want to do that extra work. I wasn't interested in graduating early. All I care about is writing.

I'm completely involved in a great conversation at the table behind me when my mother has to interfere.

"Kitty, behave yourself." She grabs my arm and drags me around to face our table.

"Are you disturbing that lady at the table behind us?" she whispers.

"No, she just asked me a question. What do you want?"

"You aren't paying any attention to our own conversation," my mom says. "Why are you always off wool-gathering at times like this? Aren't you worried about Lee Ann? What do you think of her decision to marry Adair?"

"I think she's just trying to get out of the house because you and Dad argue all the time," I answer.

"Kitty!" I've shocked my mother. "What a thing to say. Your dad and I don't argue that much. Do we, Walter?"

"Well, I guess we do sometimes," Dad answers honestly.

"Lee Ann, be honest. Are you marrying dorky Adair just to get out of the house?" I ask.

"Duh!" she says. "And Adair isn't dorky. He's really nice."

"Maybe he's really nice because he thinks you're gonna support him for the rest of his life. But the real question is, do you love him—*really* love him, can't live without him, love him?" I ask dramatically.

"Oh Kitty, that's romance novel stuff. I love him. Why else would I marry him?"

We can all see she's angry.

"Lee, you made such good grades in high school," I say. "You could have gone to any college you wanted, but you said you were tired of school and wanted to work instead. Well, you've tried that. If you want real freedom, let's talk college. Think about it: Mom and Dad will never know what time you get home, if you're out partying all night or how many guys you're dating. As long as you get good grades and don't get into any trouble, everything will be fine."

"Kitty!" Mom is in shock again. "Is that what you think college is like? Well, let me tell you, young lady. It's hard work, it's challenging. It's about learning to grow up."

I'm so relieved when I see my brother Gordon walk toward us.

"Look who's here, Mom!" I shout.

Everyone says, "Hi, Gordon," in unison.

"Gordon, Lee Ann has decided to get married," my mother whines.

"So, that's the crisis," Gordon says. "Good God, hopefully not to Adair."

I can't help but giggle.

"What's wrong with Adair?" Lee Ann asks.

"Did he finally get a job?" Gordon responds.

"No, and I don't care about that." Lee pouts.

"Well, you will. I suggest you two live together for a few years and see if he ever gets a job. That way you won't have to go through an expensive divorce when you realize he's a lazy bum," Gordon smiles.

"I think she's just doing it so she won't have to listen to Mom and Dad argue anymore," I chime in.

"Well duh! Why do you think I moved out?" he says, smiling.

"Gordon! Why would you say such a thing?" my mother moans.

"Oh, Mom, I'm just kidding." He backtracks, as usual.

I glare at him and Lee Ann hides her smile.

"Mom, are you happy?" I lean forward and ask her.

"What does that have to do with whether Lee Ann should be getting married?" She is really annoyed with me now.

"Mom, are you happy—truly happy? Do you look forward to every day? Are you excited about tomorrow?" I ask seriously.

"Yes, no, I don't know. I don't think like that, Kitty. You ask the strangest questions." She shakes her head and sighs.

"Mom, Dad, all three of us kids know that you love us," I say. "And a long time ago, you decided to stay together for our sake. And you have been great parents, really great. You've attended all of our school functions, plays, choir, sports events, everything. But you really don't like each other very much and you fight all the time."

My two siblings are looking at the floor. As usual, no help there.

"Mom, have you ever thought of getting a divorce? Dad, how about you?"

"No!" Mom says with authority. "Kitty, we are here to talk about Lee Ann, not your dad and me."

"In September, you and Dad will be empty nesters," I say. "We'll all be gone. You are both fairly young. Maybe it's time you started thinking about yourselves. And getting back to Lee Ann, wouldn't you rather see her in college than have a son-in-law who can never hold down a job? Mom, you could finally travel more. And Dad, you could do a lot more sailing."

Everyone begins to talk at once, and I'm free to go back to people watching. I've done my part. I planted the seeds. Now, as usual, it's up to Gordon to close the deal.

I don't remember how old I was when I first decided to "speak truth to power." I don't even remember what I said that day, but I'll never forget the reaction. My mother turned beet red and said, "Walter, I believe Kitty is psychologically unbalanced. We have to take her for a mental evaluation."

Horrified, Lee Ann and I turned to our older brother, Gordon, who was almost ten years older than Lee Ann and always ran interference between us and our parents. Thankfully, he just laughed and said, "Mom, I admit Kitten can be a little odd sometimes, but I would describe that as her just being extremely precocious."

I guess my parents decided having a precocious child was preferable to having a mentally unstable one. So, they let it drop.

The night after that trauma, Gordon came to my bedroom to check on me. When he came in, he said, "You know our parents just don't understand you, Kitten. It's them, not you. Tonight went well. We work good together. We should try that more often."

And we have.

Things at home have gotten worse since Dad sold his business for a bundle and Mom decided to quit her job. I guess they didn't realize the amount of stress more togetherness would put on their relationship. I know Lee Ann doesn't love Adair; she just wants out. I'd already called Gordon and filled him in.

I wonder if I should become a reporter. I'd love to interview all the different people sitting at each table—the older lady by the window who looks kind of lonely, the beautiful woman in the tight red dress who looks like a paid escort, or the couple with the little boy who just put his napkin on his head.

Maybe when I grow up, I'll write a book about them.

Things at the table behind me are getting intense. I am practicing my flirting skills when my mother once again interferes.

"Kitty!"

"Yes, mother." I say.

"You're more interested in the table behind us than your own family," she says. "But that's okay. Gordon, as usual, has solved everything. He talked Lee Ann into going to college. He's taking her on a tour of a couple of campuses next week and he thinks she may be able to register for the spring semester."

"Oh, what a good idea!"

"And for your information, your dad and I are not getting a divorce. I don't know where you get those strange ideas. Gordon wants to take us to look at some townhouse not far from the yacht club. He thinks the house might be too much for us, since it's two stories, and all."

"He has a point, Mom," I agree.

"And I never thought about us living closer to the yacht club, Kitty," my dad says, smiling.

"That sure would be convenient if you ever wanted to go on one of those sailing trips to Mexico with your friends," I encourage him.

"Oh, I don't know about that. But maybe," Dad says.

"And I was telling mom, the folks at my church have a travel club, one for couples and one just for ladies. She might come to church with me next Sunday to meet some of them," Gordon says.

"Well, we'll see," my mom says.

"And what about you, kitty cat?" Gordon asks. "Any thought about where you want to go in September? Want to come with me and Lee to visit some campuses?"

"No thanks. I've already been accepted into three schools and offered two scholarships," I say.

"Wow! Have you made a choice yet?" Gordon looks really surprised.

"Yeah, I'm going to Cornell," I tell him.

"Do you know anyone else who's going there?"

"No, not really." I shake my head.

"Lordy girl, you did all that on your own?" His eyes are wide with surprise.

I smile and say, "Yeah, you know me, Gordon. I'm different."

Anthony

I UNLOCK THE FRONT DOOR OF THE RESTAURANT AND SEND THE STAFF ON their way. They rush out into the cold and rainy weather, bundled up in coats and scarves. Re-locking the door behind them, I watch them say their goodnights, breaking up into twos and threes and hurrying off in different directions. I take a moment to watch the rain and note what little traffic there is at this time of night. I savor a deep sense of satisfaction. We have a good crew—hardworking and pretty reliable.

Walking through the bar first, I check for anything out of place. Nick's a good bartender, keeps his space neat and clean. But I have a feeling I'll be losing him soon. Nick is young, good looking, and likes the ladies. I'm surprised he's lasted this long. I should probably keep an eye out for a replacement.

Next, I head into the dining room, still checking along the way. Our staff is good at straightening up at night, but you can't be too careful. The cleaning crew will arrive early in the morning and the place will be in perfect shape when we reopen.

The new waitress, Kelly, has been a good addition to the staff. She's hard working, reliable and easy on the eye. I've noticed Nick hitting on her lately. Tonight, as they left, Nick was trying to talk her into going out, but I'm not really worried. She's a sensible girl, working on her degree. She can handle Nick. But if it gets out of hand, I'll step in.

I'm going to have to speak to Frankie in the morning. This is the third Saturday night she hasn't shown up, and she didn't even bother to call in tonight. She's been with me a long time, and I'd hate to lose her. But it isn't fair to the others to let this slide. I can't let her get away with not even calling in. I'll have to make sure she isn't having trouble at home.

Louis walks out from the back storage room.

"Are they all gone?" he asks.

"Yeah, I'm just checking things."

"I know, I took a walk through, too." He smiles.

I smile in return. We go through this routine every night.

"Is there any fresh coffee? Let's go in the back to my office," I say.

Leaving the dining room, I duck into the kitchen, even though I don't have to worry about Chef Alex's domain. He runs a tight ship—keeps the kitchen immaculate and controls waste. I wonder what happened tonight, though. Two of our workers walked off the job. I hope it wasn't because of Alex. He is a great chef, but unfortunately, he has an obnoxious personality. Tonight, he seemed agitated. He kept the yelling to a minimum, but something was wrong. If Alex wasn't such a gem, I would probably have fired him months ago. He's good, but if our workers are starting to walk off the job, I've got to find out why.

I enter the office and sit down at my desk. Louis places a cup of black decaf coffee in front of me and then one for himself across the desk.

"I wonder what was going on at the end of the street earlier," I say, feeling uneasy. "There were several police cars, lots of flashing lights. This neighborhood is really quiet; it's unusual to see such a commotion. I hope a criminal element isn't moving in around here. It would be bad for business."

"I haven't heard anything about an increase in crime, but I'll keep an ear out." Louis replies.

"Do you know anything about what happened in the kitchen tonight? We had two workers walk out on us. I asked the staff but nobody would say anything."

"The new waiter, Liam, told me there was a problem in the kitchen, so I walked in and noticed right away that Carlos was gone. Miguel was in Carlos's spot, assisting Alex. Alex, right away, started yelling at me, telling me if we didn't get him extra help in the kitchen by tomorrow, he wasn't going to show up."

Louis takes a sip of his coffee, then continues, "Man, he pissed me off. I told him if he didn't show up tomorrow, you would see to it that he didn't work in any other restaurant in the city, maybe even the state. I said, 'Remember that convention Anthony went to in New York? He's a bigwig in that organization and he can ruin your career.' I asked Jose if his two cousins could help out again tomorrow, and he said they would. At least Alex admitted that Miguel did a good job."

"So, basically you lied to Alex," I laugh.

"You're damn right, I did. Him threatening to quit when we have that big party tomorrow."

I can tell Louis is really mad.

"You live over by Miguel, don't you? Do you think he'd talk to you?" I ask.

"I'll try to talk to him tomorrow," Louis says, "but I know the problem. It's Chef Alex. He treats everyone badly. I've walked in there when his back was to me and he thought I was just one of the wait staff. The way he treats the Mexicans is the worst, and they work the hardest."

"Why didn't you tell me? You know I'd never want any of my employees to be mistreated." I try not to sound annoyed, but I am. My parents were immigrants and I won't tolerate Alex abusing them.

"You've had enough on your plate lately. I was gonna bring it up after the holidays. That's the best time to look for a new chef."

"Do you know what happened to the couple with the little boy? I was just about to go over to talk to them when I noticed they were gone. Who sat them at the table over in the corner like that?" I change the subject.

"I had gone in the back looking for the wine they said was missing, and while I was gone, the new guy sat them over there. He thought we didn't like kids coming into the restaurant on Saturday nights," Louis says.

"I hope you set him straight," I say. "I wish we could contact the couple. I really had a good laugh when the kid put his napkin on his head. Made me think of Rickie, when he was little." I smile.

"Speaking of Rickie—a full scholarship, no less!" Louis laughs.

"I know. I'm so proud of him. I really screwed it up at first." I run my hands through my hair.

"You should have called him back and apologized for hanging up on him." Louis shakes his head.

"I know, I know. And then he just walks right into my office, doesn't even knock. I was so pissed. And then he's 'We can do this the easy way or the hard way.' Like we're in a God damn movie or something. I almost started to laugh but I realized he was right. He's not a kid anymore. We're sending him off to school to act all grown up and I didn't treat him like a man. And then he hits me with the full scholarship, wanting to be closer to home. I felt about two feet tall." I pick up my pencil and start tapping it on the desk.

"Good, you deserved it," Louis smiles.

"Thanks a lot. Now I owe Dominick a big thanks and an apology. For a minute there, I thought he went behind my back and talked to Rickie all these years about being a lawyer and going to his alma mater. I really got my feelings hurt." I stop the tapping.

"It really didn't sound like something Dominick would do, but I didn't know if Rickie had secretly wanted to be a lawyer, either," Louis says.

"And then the news about Carmen!" I say. "I have to be honest. I knew she always loved working at the restaurant, but it never crossed my mind that she'd want to take over after we retire. It's always been all about Rickie. Did you know, Louis?" I ask.

"No, I'm like you. I figured she'd go off to college, meet some nice guy, get married and have a bunch of kids. I never pictured her playing a role in the business." He shakes his head again.

"I never thought of myself as being sexist. But I completely overlooked my own daughter in favor of my son. Rickie said she's already researching colleges that teach restaurant management." I frown.

"God help us when she graduates! And God help Rickie. She's always been a force to be reckoned with, ever since she learned to talk. I think Rickie is right; we're gonna need two Tony's or she'll go to work for our competition and whip our asses."

Louis and I enjoy a good laugh. I can always count on him to make me feel better.

"Bring her with you early tomorrow morning," he says. "We can use an extra pair of hands in case Frankie is still out, and it's time we start training her. She's old enough to bus tables this summer."

"You're right. Thanks Louis. It's getting late, you better get going. I'll see you tomorrow." I smile.

"Goodnight, boss," he says.

The restaurant was crowded tonight; the typical Saturday night crowd; standing room only at the bar. I'm sure the take will be lucrative.

I'm just finishing the bookkeeping when my phone rings. Maria rarely calls me, and I hope nothing is wrong. I hope Rickie got home okay.

I pick up. "Hello?"

"Hey Anthony, this is Maria's cousin, Joey," the caller says. "Maria said I could probably still catch you there. Do you have some time to talk?"

"Yeah, I guess so. What's up?" I say.

"Well, you know my brother Michael who had a heart attack, right?" Joey says.

"Yes, Maria keeps me informed. She said he's doing great."

"Yeah, he is, but you know his son Mike Jr.?" he asks.

"Sure, he worked for me here at the restaurant when he was in high school."

"Well, you know he moved to New York and became a big chef in a fancy hotel there, won all kinds of awards," Joey says.

"Sure, I've followed his career. I'm proud of him. He once told me working here is what made him want to be a chef. How is he doing?"

"Well, he wants to move back home and be close to his parents. They're getting older and with his dad having the heart attack, and all. So I was hoping maybe you could put the word out that he's looking for a job," Joey says.

"Well, I don't have any connections with the big hotels downtown but I'll call around and see what I can do. I'll help in any way I can."

"Mike said he's interested in anything. He's kind of had it with the big-name restaurants, said the pressure can be murder."

"Really? Is he in New York or is he still in town?" I ask.

"Still here, staying with his folks."

"Tell Mike I'll stop by tomorrow morning. I might have something he would be interested in. If I'm in a bind, I might even have to ask him for a favor."

"I'll call Mike as soon as I hang up. Thanks, Anthony. Michael has an appointment with his doctor on Monday. If the doctor releases him to get out and about again, he and Ann Marie want us to bring them by for dinner."

"Okay, Joey. I'll make sure Maria is here, too. I'll reserve the best table in the house. See you then."

The rain and the wind have really picked up, and I'm anxious to get home. Maria will probably have coffee and pie waiting for me. We have a lot to talk about tonight.

I'm sure she'll want to hear all about my meeting with Rickie, probably word for word. We'll need to talk about Carmen. I want to ask Maria if she knew about our daughter's dream to take over the business and if she did, why she never told me. And I have to ask Maria if she feels that I have treated our daughter unfairly. I have to say, I'm dreading the answer to that question.

I pull my collar closer around my neck and hurry to my car. I have lots of exciting news of my own to share about the restaurant: Frankie not showing up for work again, the problems in the kitchen, two workers walking out, Chef Alex's threatening not to show up tomorrow, and her cousin Michael's son looking for a job.

Fortunately, inside the restaurant itself, this was the best kind of night—the kind where absolutely nothing out of the ordinary happened.

Acknowledgements

Over twenty years ago, my daughter-in-law, Marilyn Carle, recommended a writing class taught once a month at the Spectrum Center. "Everybody raves about the teacher," she said.

My son added, "If you want to take the classes, Mom, I'll pay for them." I considered that an offer I couldn't refuse. I thought it would be a great opportunity to write some amusing stories about raising my four wonderful children.

The first prompt given in class was, "Write how an extraordinary day was also ordinary." I began writing, and soon I was sniffling, then crying. Next, snot began running out of my nostrils. I was so embarrassed, yet grateful, when another student handed me a box of tissues.

The teacher explained that each student could voluntarily read their work, and afterward, we would take a break. I was convinced that if I read, during the break the moderator would suggest that I really should take painting lessons.

As my turn grew nearer, I began to sweat.

The teacher asked, "Barbara, would you like to read?"

I answered, "I'll try."

"Mom, I have cancer," I read. "Those four words led my son and I on a journey that lasted less than two years."

When I finished reading, the teacher said, "Wow! You have an important story to tell that no one but you can write."

That was the day I met Max Regan, my teacher, my coach, my

developmental editor and my dear friend. He has taught me so much. He encouraged me—then pushed me—to send my work out into the world. I never would have achieved anything without Max.

The day he said, "I think it's time you should try to publish your work," my response was, "I'm not good enough."

When he encouraged me to start reading my work to the public, my response was, "What?!"

His faith in me never faltered.

In that same class, I wrote a short piece about a woman sitting all alone in a restaurant. A few months later, I wrote another one about a couple sitting at a table at this same location. That day, a small seed was planted in the back of my brain that if I wrote more of these, I might have a book.

One year, while attending Max's ten-day writer's retreat in Boulder, Colorado, I shared a house with two very talented, young writers. We discussed how all of us were working on more than one project. I mentioned the stories that kept popping up about this restaurant. One of the women—Fern Brady—said, "I'm a publisher, and I'd be interested in a book like that."

Over the years, while I struggled writing the memoirs about my son Scott, I'd run into Fern, and she always asked, "How's that book coming?"

Class after class, here and there, I'd add another tale.

This is where I'm supposed to recognize all of you who assisted me with your support and helpful critiques. Unfortunately, after so many classes and years, I can't possibly remember all of your names. If I have missed acknowledging you, please forgive me.

Many thanks to the amazing Rosa Glenn Reilly, the director of the Spectrum Center and my dear friend for over twenty years, and to the members of the Spectrum Writer's Guild—Melanie Miller Ormond, Ellen Seaton, Diana Galindo, Kay Cox, Kirsten Cerre and Ron Buecker—for their thoughtful suggestions and gentle critiques.

Also, the group of writers that meet in Rosa's office, known as The Tree House, and especially the talented Tina Borja, who left us way too soon, as well as Ed Gumnick and Crosby Bean.

The late, dear Pat Clark then founded another group, The Wednesday Morning Writers, with Diana Galindo, Rosa Glenn Reilly, Melanie Miller Ormond, and Ellen Seaton, together with Suzan Cotellesse,

Rose Niles, and myself. I will always be grateful for their years of encouragement and professional suggestions.

Thanks also to my Parklane Fan Club—Ruth Stevenson, Barbara Ragland, Pam Brown and Carol Wolf—who have listened to my work and offered honest feedback. And to Carol Wolf and Rhonda Hassenbusch for being my beta readers.

Of course, I have to give special thanks to my dear friend Fern Brady, who never stopped asking about that book. When my memoirs were finished, I called her and said, "I finally finished." We meet for lunch regularly, and she is now my publisher.

But no acknowledgement would be complete without thanking my fabulous family. My three children, Paula, Melissa and Glen, have attended so many of my readings and listened to my first drafts. My two most supportive grandchildren, Rose Carle and Scott McDaniel, who are always interested in my latest plot twists. But most of all, my wonderful husband Ed, who for sixty-four years has supported me in anything I decided to try: painting classes, pottery classes, tennis lessons, and finally, writing classes. He has driven me to readings all over the state of Texas, and has listened to and read my work. He's honest enough to tell me when and where my story lines need work. So, on occasion, he's even become my partner in crime.

Biography

Barbara Ann Carle is an essayist, poet, and novelist. Her essays have appeared in numerous anthologies including, *Fearless Nest, That Thing You Do, Thanksgiving to Christmas, A Patchwork of Stories* and five *Chicken Soup* books.

Barbara's poems have appeared in various publications including the 2009 Poetry Society of Texas – Book of the Year, the 2011, 20112 and 2013 Texas Poetry Calendars, the 2012 Summer Edition of *Rattle Magazine* and the 2016 Mutabilis Press anthology *Untameable City.* Two of her poetry books have been published *New York Rhapsody* in 2009 and *Cave Drawings* in 2017.

A collection of essays about the loss of her son Scott, *The Viking Ship* was published in 2018. Barbara is busy doing the final edits of her latest novel *Murder on Delivery* which should be available in early 2024.

She is a member of Gulf Coast Poets, The Poetry Society of Texas, Women in the Visual and Literary Arts and The Houston Writer's Guild.

Barbara was born and raised in Brooklyn, New York. She has been a Texas transplant since 1965 when she and her family relocated to Houston for the Space Program. Barbara is the mother of four, the grandmother of seven and great-grandmother of one. She and her husband of sixty-four years, Ed, presently live in a high-rise in downtown Houston.

Made in the USA
Middletown, DE
16 March 2024

50978060R10085